Li Jun and the IRON ROAD

Li Jun and the IRON ROAD

Anne Tait
with Paulette Bourgeois

Based on the screen story by Barry Pearson and screenplay by Barry Pearson and Raymond Storey

DUNDURN
TORONTO

Based on the screen story by Barry Pearson and screenplay by Barry Pearson and Raymond Storey

Editor: Cheryl Hawley
Design: Laura Boyle
Cover Design: Laura Boyle
Cover images © Anne Tait
Printer: Webcom

Library and Archives Canada Cataloguing in Publication

Tait, Anne, author
Li Jun and the iron road / Anne Tait ; with Paulette Bourgeois.

Issued in print and electronic formats.

ISBN 978-1-4597-3142-4 (pbk.).--ISBN 978-1-4597-3143-1 (pdf).
--ISBN 978-1-4597-3144-8 (epub)

1. Iron Road (Television program)--Juvenile fiction. I. Bourgeois, Paulette, author II. Title.

PS8639.A35L5 2015 jC813'.6 C2015-900595-7
C2015-900596-5

1 2 3 4 5 19 18 17 16 15

Canada Council
for the Arts
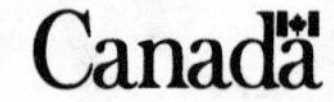

We acknowledge the support of the **Canada Council for the Arts** and the **Ontario Arts Council** for our publishing program. We also acknowledge the financial support of the **Government of Canada** through the **Canada Book Fund** and **Livres Canada Books**, and the **Government of Ontario** through the **Ontario Book Publishing Tax Credit** and the **Ontario Media Development Corporation**.

Printed and bound in Canada.

Visit us at

Dundurn.com | *@dundurnpress* | *Facebook.com/dundurnpress* | *Pinterest.com/dundurnpress*

Dundurn
3 Church Street, Suite 500
Toronto, Ontario, Canada
M5E 1M2

To the thousands of Chinese workers who died building our railway — three for every mile of track they laid

ACKNOWLEDGEMENTS

Thanks to Barry Pearson and Raymond Storey for their wonderful screenplay, to Marjorie Lamb for her writing and editing contributions, to John Millyard for notes and support, to Arnie Zipursky and everyone at CCI Entertainment and to Raymond Massey of MPL for invaluable help in getting the film onto the screen, and to Patrick Boyer for getting the book into print. Thanks to Tapestry for the inspiration of their opera, to David Wu for his brilliant direction of the film *Iron Road*, to its many funders including Telefilm Canada, CMF, CBC, the Harold Greenberg Fund, Cogeco, the Shaw Rocket Fund, and to REEL Canada for their many screenings of it across Canada.

We also wish to thank writers Paul Yee and Arlene Chan, as well as Kangmei Wang and the staff at the Far Eastern Library of the Royal Ontario Museum, for expanding our understanding of the experiences of the

Chinese people in Canada and China. *The Last Spike* by Pierre Berton and *Blood and Iron, Building the Railway* by Paul Yee were very helpful in our research.

Note to the Reader

Many of the events and some of the characters in this book are drawn from history, but this is a work of fiction — a what-if story — and some historical details have been altered. The characters' names are in Mandarin, as mandated for the film *Iron Road*, but most of the Chinese phrases are in Cantonese because the railway workers spoke Taishanese and Cantonese. In the film, all the Chinese dialogue is subtitled and Li Jun speaks English with an accent. In the novel, when Li Jun speaks with other Chinese people their Chinese dialogue is written as fluent English. When she talks to James, Edgar, or other Westerners, her dialogue is in limited English.

Chapter One

The rooster in the Ho household's courtyard crowed loudly to greet the dawn and the caged birds in the kitchen answered with sweet, high melodies. Li Jun stretched and yawned, warmed by the first rays of sun streaming through the tiny window in her servant's quarters. *Such a glorious day*, she thought. Then she remembered — in moments she'd be summoned by First Wife screeching like a cat in a sack about to be drowned. For the past three long years, Li Jun had wakened to the same opera.

And there it was again: "Lazy girl! Come here! My chamber pot is full and the stink is making me green."

"Coming, Mistress. I will bring your breakfast," she would always answer.

Li Jun splashed water on her face, quickly twisted her waist-length hair into two braids that she coiled around her ears, pulled on her trousers and jacket. Darn! There was a stain on her sleeve. She spat on her finger and dabbed at the stain but it didn't change — still dark and greasy. Muttering to herself, she ran from her room on the far side of the courtyard to the main house. Until she arrived in Hong Kong as a twelve-year-old country girl to work as a *mui jai*, a "little sister," she'd never seen such wealth, never imagined room upon room filled with carved wooden furniture, floors polished to a sheen, thick carpets everywhere, and gas lamps glowing in the dining room at night. But that was three years ago and back then she also never imagined that *she* would be the one on her hands and knees polishing those floors and washing the fine china until the skin on her hands was raw. The worst of her jobs? Reaching under the Ho family beds every morning to remove their chamber pots and empty them onto the garden vegetables. She plugged her nose and chewed on a piece of mint from the garden to keep from gagging, then washed the pots until they gleamed.

Cook was busy in the kitchen when Li Jun came to fetch First Wife's breakfast. On the tray was a bowl of steaming congee, plump with fish and pickled vegetables, plus a pot of jasmine tea. Li Jun was tempted to dip her finger into the porridge for just a taste — it looked so appetizing and her stomach ached with hunger. But later she would eat *her* breakfast of cold rice and maybe, if Cook was in a good mood, he'd throw in a mouthful of wilted greens.

First Wife squawked from her bedroom even more loudly. Cook winced and motioned Li Jun to head upstairs.

"How do you stand it, day after day?" she asked him.

He hesitated. "She wasn't always this bad. In fact, she was happy until she found she couldn't have children. Mr. Ho wanted a son, so he found Second Wife. Now First Wife is miserable with everyone."

Second Wife was big in the belly soon after coming to the house and gave birth to a son. First Wife wanted to send her away and raise the boy as her own but Mr. Ho had his own reasons for keeping Second Wife around. She was not much older than Li Jun, dainty and very pretty, and she warmed his bed most nights. Li Jun had scant sympathy for the tyrant upstairs. Still, she thought it was sad that First Wife had no children and her husband had brought a woman half her age with twice her beauty into her house.

She knew that *her* father, far away in Gold Mountain, was faithful to her mother. They had been strangers on their wedding night, as in most arranged marriages, but love had blossomed and Li Jun remembered how tender they were with one another.

In all her time as a servant girl, not a day passed that Li Jun didn't long to be back with her family in her cottage by the river in Ping Wei. It had been a simple life full of joy and abundance. Her father, Li Man, taught at the village school; her mother, Shuqin, farmed the fields and tended to the house and garden. Li Jun was a carefree child then, but now it all seemed like a dream, a lifetime ago.

Terrible things happened all over Guangdong. Li Man led the local farmers in their revolt against the brutal and greedy Manchu warlords, but lost the battle and his teaching job and in revenge they burned down his house. Then drought hit the village. Their crops failed and they faced starvation. Li Man decided the only way to avoid disaster was to go off to "Gold Mountain" in America. There he would search for gold — they said it was lying in the ditches. There he would make his fortune and keep his family alive. He would send money every month, and when he was rich he would come back to them.

At first his letters arrived full of love and longing, with enough money to support the two of them. Then, mysteriously, the letters stopped and there was nothing they could ...

Enough! Li Jun chided herself. *Stop daydreaming and get to work.* She was at First Wife's door now. She knocked gently on it and carefully balanced the tray as she entered. But a gust of wind slammed the door shut behind her with a resounding THUD. First Wife, startled by the noise, jumped up in her bed, pulled back her quilt, and lifted a thick, dimpled leg over the side, balancing precariously on one elbow and groaning with the effort of sitting up.

"Wait! I'll help you," cried Li Jun, setting the tray down on the ornate dresser. But no — she was too late. First Wife kicked over her chamber pot and the fetid contents pooled in a disgusting mess by the bed.

"You stupid girl! This is your fault for slamming that door. And what's this? There's a spot on your sleeve. Such a dirty *mui jai!* Your mother would be ashamed."

You know nothing of my family! Li Jun wanted to shout. *How dare you degrade me? My father was a teacher, a brave man with a fire in his soul to do what was right! My mother was proud of me. Didn't I give up everything — the chance for school, for a husband — to come here to work for you, you fat cow?* But instead she clamped her lips together, took a deep breath, and bowed to her mistress. More than anything, Li Jun knew she must be obedient. She'd heard what happened to uppity servants. Long ago when a cook's helper spoke back to First Wife, his back was caned to a bloody pulp.

As she wiped up the spill and scrubbed the floor, she had only one thought: *the old cow was right when she said her chamber pot made her feel green. Her shit did stink more than most.*

More than ever, Li Jun wished she was at home. She would never forget the day her world changed forever. It was her twelfth birthday and her mother had scrounged enough to buy the rarest of treats — a bean cake. Li Jun took a bite and swooned with the pleasure at the first taste of the sweet paste. There had been no sweets for a long time. Not since a year before, at Chinese New Year, when they received a letter from her father, along with most of his wages from the past months. He wrote that the gold rush in America was over, so he was travelling north to British Columbia, the new Gold Mountain, to find work. There was still gold in those rivers and a railway was being built right across Canada from the Pacific to the Atlantic coasts.

It was a long letter, full of excitement. Canada was a new Dominion, no longer under direct rule of Britain. Many people in British Columbia wanted to join the United States but the first prime minister of Canada promised them an iron road, a railway that would link the vast nation from sea to sea. It was a big country, Li Man wrote, even bigger than the ocean he had crossed from China to the new world! The railway lines in the east were nearly finished but building the western track through the forests and mountains of British Columbia was so dangerous that it was way behind schedule. Li Man wrote that a powerful contractor was hiring Chinese workers to clear the land, blast tunnels through rock, and lay the track in the Rocky Mountains. He was excited by his prospects and promised his wife and daughter that once he was settled up in Canada, he would send lots of money back to them. That was his last letter. Li Jun and her mother read it over every day, as they waited for more news and the promised money. But that never came.

Li Jun offered a bite of her bean cake to Shuqin, who shook her head and smiled as her daughter devoured the birthday gift. But Li Jun was worried. Her mother's eyes were dark as stone, and purple half moons had settled into deep hollows underneath them. She took her hand. "Have you had bad news from Father?"

Shuqin ignored the question. "Is the cake good?" she asked. Li Jun was not a child; she knew her mother was hiding something dreadful.

"He's dead, isn't he?"

Her mother sighed and looked away as if gathering her strength to answer. "Li Jun, I don't know. He hasn't sent money in more than a year. He doesn't write. There must be some explanation. Your father is a good man. He's brave too. He would never abandon us. But look at you — you're little more than skin stretched over bones. We're starving. The roof is broken, and when the rains come it will fall in and we have no money to fix it."

Li Jun had an idea. "I'll quit school and sell our vegetables in the market."

"Sweet girl, we don't have enough vegetables to feed *ourselves,* never mind sell to others. Besides, it's too dangerous here now. Every day I hear of another girl kidnapped and sold as a slave … or worse."

Li Jun pretended she didn't know what *worse* meant, but she did. Everyone in the village talked. Girls were stolen, then beaten and forced into brothels to please men with their bodies. They were never seen again.

Li Jun felt her stomach churn as her mother continued. "The head of our clan has made me an offer we cannot refuse. You will become a *mui jai* in Hong Kong for Mr. Ho. He is a rich man who needs help with his son and his two wives."

"A little sister?" said Li Jun. She understood exactly what that meant. She would be loaned to the Ho family as a servant. Her mother would get money, enough to survive, in exchange for her servitude. She forced back her tears and stifled the urge to scream: "NO!" She had no choice but to accept her mother's decision. It was her duty.

"It won't be for long, Li Jun," said her mother gently. "Once your father returns, he will pay back the debt to Mr. Ho, we will be a family again, and we will find you a good husband."

The next day, as she embraced her mother and said goodbye, Li Jun made herself a promise. She would not be a servant forever. She would find another way to support the two of them. She was like her father — brave. And there was a fire burning in her soul, too.

WHOMP! A fan hit her on the head. She put up both hands to protect herself from First Wife's anger.

"Pay attention, stupid girl! Take away my tray and lay out my clothes. I am meeting with my mah-jong group this afternoon and I plan to look particularly fetching as I take all the winnings."

Li Jun snapped back to the present. To make First Wife look "fetching" would take much more than the fanciest silk dress. It would take a miracle.

Chapter Two

By late afternoon Li Jun had done the work of ten servants. The more she did, the more First and Second Wife found for her to do. She still hadn't had time to wash her own jacket so the stain remained as a sign that no matter what she did for her mistresses, there was no time to take care of herself. And now she had to attend to the mending.

Through the open window of the study on the far side of the courtyard, she heard the voices of Mr. Ho's only son, little Ho Kwong, and his tutor. Li Jun felt a weight lift from her shoulders. She adored the boy. He was just like the little brother she'd always wanted: quick and mischievous, with a good heart. He stole sweet cakes for her and left them, wrapped in paper, in her laundry basket. She would pinch his cheeks and chase him down the halls, threatening to tickle him, and she found ways to time her chores so she could sit in the courtyard beneath the library window to do her mending during his lessons.

She had a reason: through the window she could listen to Little Kwong's lessons and watch as he practised his writing. Her father had taught her to read and given her a writing slate. It was one of the few things she'd brought with her from the country. Each day she watched Little Kwong write the elaborate characters on his blackboard; each night she wrote them from memory on her slate and thought of her father — how he would slap his thigh and praise her smallest successes. She hoped he would be proud of her for continuing to learn on her own.

Learning Chinese reading and writing was more difficult than she'd remembered. There were more than five thousand Chinese characters to master but she proved to be a quick study. There were English lessons too. Mr. Ho boasted that he was so successful as a trade merchant because he could bargain with the foreigners in their language and he wanted his son to have the same advantages. But English was much more difficult for Li Jun — all those foreign sounds rolled around her mouth like marbles.

When she ran into Little Kwong after his lesson, she would try out new phrases.

"Ha — do — you — do, Master Kwong?"

Little Kwong clapped his hands with delight. "How do — *you* — do?" he answered. "I am fine!"

When no one was watching, he would slip her a piece of chalk. "To practise your writing," he said, and Li Jun flashed one of her rare smiles.

"Why do you want to learn?" asked the little boy.

"To honour my father by being first class!"

Kwong looked at her strangely. "Don't tell my father that I help you. He will be angry. He says servants should do much and know little."

After her supper of rice and steamed bok choy, Li Jun said a weary good night to Cook and stumbled sleepily into the courtyard. She closed her eyes as she walked, concentrating on her English and repeating out loud, "How-do-you-do? I am fine."

Suddenly she was aware that she wasn't alone. She stopped and looked into the darkness, heard the strike of a match, and saw the red glow of a cigar being inhaled. Smoke curled into the cool air. By the light of a waning moon she saw Mr. Ho standing under the banyan tree in the centre of the yard, smoking, his gaze focused intently on her. She felt trapped — like the prey of a tiger about to pounce. Her skin crawled and she wanted to run as far as she could, but there was nowhere to go.

"Come here, Little Sister," he ordered. She'd never heard him speak this way — in a rough, breathy voice. Her heart beat wildly but she wouldn't let him know she was afraid. She walked toward him, as she always did before her master: demurely, with her head bowed, her hands clasped, taking tiny steps as if her feet were bound like the empress dowager.

She stood in front of him, eyes downcast.

"So, you are learning English," he snarled. "Such ambitions for a *mui jai*! I've underestimated you. And you are quite grownup now, aren't you?"

He grabbed her arm and pulled her into him. His breath was hot, smoky, and foul. She turned her head to the side but he pinched her chin and forced her face upward so that she had no choice but to look into his greedy eyes. He forced his mouth on hers and ran his hands over her breasts.

A door slammed. Cook dumped a bucket of water onto the herbs in the courtyard and called out, "Who's there?"

Li Jun wanted to shout, *It's me, Little Sister. Help me!* but she was trapped. No one could help her. Mr. Ho held her in the shadow of the tree, hidden from Cook's view, and raised his fist in a threat. Then he emerged from the shadow, blowing smoke rings into the air.

"Just me," he answered. "Having a smoke."

Cook bowed, said good night, and headed back to the kitchen.

Mr. Ho reached for Li Jun once more. He tickled her chin and laughed as she cringed at his touch.

"Go to bed now," he commanded. "I can have you any time I want. I own you."

She wanted to spit in his pockmarked face.

As she made her way across the courtyard, she heard a noise from the family quarters. Standing at the window was Second Wife, watching.

Days passed and Li Jun managed to stay a distance from her boss. She walked on the other side of the hall whenever their paths crossed but she knew it wouldn't be long before he cornered her again.

Second Wife scolded her at every turn and once she turned on her. "You dirty *mui jai*," she sneered, "if I ever find you again with Mr. Ho, your life will be worthless."

Li Jun had no one to confide in and at night she fell into restless sleep, tearing at her covers, praying for a sign that her destiny was not to become the concubine of a slobbering old man. It would be better to be dead.

She thought her ancestors had heard her when a messenger came from her village. But it was hardly the news she hoped to hear. He brought word that her mother was gravely ill. Could her daughter please be allowed to visit with her in her final days?

At first Mr. Ho was adamant. No, the house could not manage without her. Li Jun hung her head to hide her tears. Then she had a brilliant idea. She wiped her cheeks with her sleeve and turned to Second Wife, silently begging with her eyes. Wouldn't she want to get rid of Li Jun for a while, to regain her favoured place in the household?

Second Wife's eyes widened as if she had just been given a present. She sidled up to Mr. Ho and, in a seductive voice, pleaded with him to help the girl honour her dying mother's wish.

"This act of kindness will bring you good joss," she whispered. "Your ancestors will reward you handsomely."

A few days later, Mr. Ho stood by Li Jun as the ox cart he'd hired arrived to take her upriver to her village. He breathed heavily as he pressed coins into her hand and told her they were to pay for her mother's funeral. In spite of her hatred for him, Li Jun was grateful for the money — now she would be able to send her mother into the spirit world. She bowed three times to her master but Mr. Ho laughed.

"You may be learning English but you are not so smart. This is not a gift. You will have to pay back this money … one way or another." He grabbed her elbow and guided her onto the cart.

Li Jun did not look back.

It took her a full day to travel home along the rutted roads. Things had been harder than she imagined. The rains never came. Winds lifted the soil so that nothing grew. More wars against the ruling landlords had devastated the villages. Li Jun felt a profound sadness travelling through her countryside. Her father had been wise to go to Gold Mountain but now he was lost. And soon her mother would be too.

Inside her mother's home it was dark and the smell of sickness was suffocating. Li Jun knelt beside the bed and gasped — her beautiful mother had become a shrivelled version of herself. When she coughed, her phlegm was specked with blood. "My poor mother," Li Jun cried, putting her arms around her. "Look what's become of you. I should have been here to take care of you."

Shuqin held her daughter very close. Her hands were cold to the touch. "No. No. You went to the city so that I could survive here. You kept me alive for all these years. You were only a child when you left. Now you are a young woman. You gave your life for mine."

Li Jun trembled as her mother's voice became thin and her breaths shallow.

"One last thing, my daughter. Promise me you will go to Gold Mountain to find your father."

Reaching under her pillow, Shuqin pulled out the only memento she had of him: a tintype photo. Li Jun had never seen it before. It was a thin piece of tin etched with a family photograph of herself as a baby in her mother's arms, her father standing beside them. The image of his face was worn to a blur and Shuqin explained why. "Every night since he left I say, 'Good night, my cherished husband.' Then I touch his face as if he was here."

Li Jun lay beside her mother, cradling the photograph in her hands. "I promise, *Ama.* I will find him."

"I do not want to think this," whispered Shuqin, "but if he has died, you must bring him home to rest beside me."

She took a last shuddering breath and stared at her daughter with milky, vacant eyes. She was gone. Li Jun choked on her tears and traced her fingers over the photograph, caressing each face, until she fell asleep with her mother wrapped in her arms.

There was no family left to help her mourn her mother's death. Still, Li Jun wanted a proper burial to send her mother into the spirit world. She did the best she could: she arranged for the body to be buried, covered her mother's altar with a piece of black cloth, and hung a white cloth over the doorway, all the while her sorrow weighing like a stone on her heart. She burned incense and lit a white candle. She cried out mournful wails to her ancestors to remove any obstacles in her mother's journey to the afterlife, then she bowed and burned joss paper so that her mother would have a rich life there.

After the burial, Li Jun stayed in her mother's house for seven days. She tried to remember their happy times together, cooking and gardening. For brief moments she smiled at those memories but soon she fell into a dark place, knowing that she would never laugh with her mother again.

She had never felt more alone or confused and she faced an urgent dilemma: how could she actually find her father? That would take money, lots of it, for the passage to Gold Mountain. How could she ever pay for the long trip across the ocean? How could she feed herself? What work could she do once she reached the New World? But returning to her life as a little sister in the Ho household was impossible. She cringed, remembering how Mr. Ho's hands snaked over her body. But if she didn't return to Mr. Ho, she had no doubt that he would track her down, beat her, and take her as his concubine. Who knew what Second Wife might do then? Li Jun struggled to remind herself that she was first class, she could think this through. She had just enough of Mr. Ho's money left to travel back to Hong Kong, but what would await her there?

She was fifteen now. Many girls her age were already married and protected by their husbands and families, but she had no one. *Think!* she admonished herself. *You need a job to get the money to find your father. What can you do?*

There were no decent jobs for women in Hong Kong. It was no secret that women on their own there were lured into brothels. They were promised money and a roof over their heads, but most of the money they earned went to their bosses, they lost their innocence and the chance to get married. These prostitutes were called *po xie*, broken shoes, and no man would marry such a woman. No, she wouldn't — couldn't — do that. Why was life so cruel for women in China?

"Men are so lucky!" she cried out, slamming her fist onto the table so hard that her teacup jumped. She ran a list through her head. Men were doted on by their mothers. They got the best clothes, the best morsels of meat and sweets, and even the poorest man expected his wife to treat him like an emperor. Men ruled the world while women emptied the chamber pots. Men got paid. Men went to Gold Mountain.

Ah! Suddenly her heart swelled with excitement and hope. She really was first class! She had the answer to her problems. It was simple, really. She would transform herself into a man and change her destiny. This way Mr. Ho would never find her and she could get a job that paid enough for her passage across the sea. She would keep her promise to her mother and find her father in Gold Mountain.

Li Jun took the photo that her mother gave her, brought it to her lips, and gave it a kiss. "Thank you, *Ama,*" she said. "Your spirit will guide me on this journey."

The next day, she took the last of her money and bought a razor, some boy's clothing, and several yards of cloth. Carefully she scraped the razor along her scalp, leaving her hair from the mid-point back to be braided into a Manchu queue. She forced herself to be stoic — she must act like a boy now and show no fear or girlish emotions. She watched her thick black hair fall onto the floor. She would bury it, along with her girlish dreams to marry and have children.

She wrapped the cloth tight around her chest, flattening her breasts, then put on the rough shirt and pants of a village boy. She practised walking with a wide-legged swagger, sitting on a three-legged stool with her legs spread, taking up the room of a man entitled to any space he wanted. Hmm … there was something missing. A hat! She pulled on a slouchy one that almost covered her eyes and in a flash of brilliance, she thought, she chewed on the end of a match. She screwed up her courage and spit out a swear word she'd heard boys use and then examined herself in the mirror. Yes, it worked!

"You are brave like your father," she told herself. "And you are fierce like a tiger."

But what would be her new name? It had to remind her of who she must be from now on. She came up close to the mirror and said, "How do you do? I am *Xiao Hu*. Little Tiger."

Chapter Three

Hong Kong, 1882

It was three years later and Chinese New Year was approaching. Little Tiger had been working from sunrise to sunset at the firework factory on the hill above Hong Kong, boxing strings of miniature crackers and fancy rockets. New Year was the factory's busiest time of year. Everyone wanted their own fireworks display to bring their families peace and prosperity in the Year of the Horse. It was a backbreaking day job with only pennies for pay, so Little Tiger looked for every chance to earn more. She picked up and delivered laundry from the Wing Laundry to the *gwailo* — the white foreigners — and her newest scheme was to buy extra fireworks from her boss at the factory and sell them for a small profit from a stall of her own in the market square. She figured that customers wouldn't mind paying a little extra for fireworks so they could buy them direct in time for New Year. To run out would be very bad luck.

She had strung her stall with all sorts of firecrackers and rockets and was calling out "Get your firecrackers here!" but her plea was drowned out by the beat of drums, signalling the start of the dragon dance in the midst of the square. She watched the dancers lift their poles to reveal a gigantic paper dragon head, as brilliantly coloured as the most spectacular of her fireworks. She marvelled at how they made the dragon's head come alive by lifting, thrusting, and dipping it as they paraded through the market. Other dancers followed right behind, lifting their poles so the dragon's body followed its head, snaking through the crowds in a slow dance as the drums banged away. Fathers lifted their children up on their shoulders to get a better look. The children screamed with terror as the dragon approached, belching smoke and fire. Little Tiger smiled at them and remembered that long ago she too had sat on *her* father's shoulders, knowing he would protect her from the dragons who danced in the parade in her village … and the ones she imagined in her mind.

Now she was all grown up, struggling to earn enough to keep her promise to find him. When she had returned to Hong Kong as a boy, she'd survived by living on the streets, sleeping in abandoned buildings, and eating garbage. She was dirty much of the time, hiding her body under wide pants and bulky, quilted jackets. She wrapped scarves around her neck to hide her girlish throat. She kept her hair shaved like most Chinese men, halfway back her head then in a long queue down her back. Always she wore her big, slouchy hat to cover much of her face. Despite her disguise, she had started keeping a knife hidden in her sleeve — just in case.

She kept to herself, afraid of getting close to anyone, lest they discover her secret. Her longing to go to Gold Mountain to search for her father was what drove her. That last letter of his had said he was heading up to Canada, to British Columbia, to work on the railway. That's where she must go to bring him home — dead or alive.

The dragon dancers passed through the market and, with a sigh, Little Tiger decided that if she was going to sell anything in this bustling crowd, she'd better wade into the sea of shoppers. She wrapped red strings of miniature snapping firecrackers around her neck and filled a basket with bundles of bigger fireworks that would rocket upward when they were lit and burst into cascades of purples and greens, sparkling brighter than stars. She set the basket on the stall table, leaned back, and pushed her arms through its straps to position it on her back. She staggered under the awkward burden and shifted the basket until she found her balance, then set off.

She weaved in and out of the crowd calling out, "Get your firecrackers here! Get them now for New Year!"

She was scanning the faces around her searching for likely buyers, when a missionary lady approached her, cloaked in black and clutching a Bible to her ample chest. Little Tiger often wondered about these strange women from distant Christian countries. They did not seem to be like Chinese women at all.

First, there was the matter of their hair. Chinese women, except for the ancient ones, had hair black as coal, fashioned neatly in buns or braids. Chinese women dressed modesty, careful to hide their slim but shapely figures under their *samfu.* Their fashions hadn't changed since the last dynasty. Even the wives of wealthy landowners wore long jackets with bell-shaped sleeves over billowing pants or skirts. The richer the wife, the more elaborate the embroidery on her jacket. However, a Chinese woman's beauty was not to be found in what she wore, but in her character and in her duty to her family. This, thought Little Tiger, was the way women *should* appear.

But the women from away? Some had hair in colours that defied imagination — red like flaming embers, yellow as summer wheat, brown like the fur of a mouse. Some of the young women let their hair flow loosely down their backs. Others piled it on top of their heads like crowns with tendrils and curls framing their faces.

And there was no modesty among these foreign women, excepting the missionaries of course. They came in different shapes and heights. Some were fleshy with mounds of fat that jiggled like custard under their long dresses. Others were lean and tall as ghostly birch trees.

But it was their clothing that set them apart from the Chinese. Most of the wives and daughters of the wealthy foreigners swished and sashayed as they took their promenades in snug silk and taffeta bodices and billowing skirts. These women pushed their breasts together and up until they looked like buns rising. They pinched

"Get your fireworks here for New Year."

She looked up at the recruiting poster — a North-West Mounted Policeman with a wide-brimmed hat and a scarlet tunic.

The bully lit the fuses and all her firecrackers exploded
WHIZ! BOOM! BANG!

The scrawny workers protested and James fired
a shot into the air.

The oarsman paddled his three passengers up to Little Tiger's home village.

"You've got big dreams," said Wang Ma, laughing aloud.

Rain was pelting down when the ship docked in Victoria Harbour, British Columbia.

Steam hit Little Tiger and Wang Ma as they arrived at the work camp.

Little Tiger was amazed by the buzz of construction all around her.

Their job was to build the railway track to Eagle Pass to connect with the track from the east.

"Be a good tea boy and stay alive," said Bookman.

"Never trust the *gwailo*," whispered Bookman.

The men killed in the tunnel were laid out along the track, with no doctors in sight.

She pulled on the gloves and squeezed herself into the oh-so-narrow hole.

Edgar lit the fuse and with a fearsome hiss, the flame travelled along it to inside the tunnel.

"It's open! I told you I explode fantastic."

Turning away from Wang Ma, she wept.

"I get it," said James. "You're nervous about going bare ass."

“I don’t want you to go either.”

Alfred Nichol hissed, “We won’t be held hostage by a bunch of superstitious Chinamen!”

He reached for her hand.
"Bring your photograph to my railcar tonight."

"Just James," he said and leaned in to kiss her.

"I bet I'm the biggest surprise you've
had this week," cooed Melanie.

“I’m a hawk!” shouted Wang Ma,
spreading his arms like wings.

“How much time do we have to set our charges?”

“I want you, and I don’t give a damn who else knows or what they think.”

Bookman leaped onto her rope. “Give me your hand!”

Li Jun stared at the photograph, then at Bookman, blood seeping from his mouth.

Li Jun knelt beside her father's funeral pyre.

“I need you to hold me one last time.”

their waists into whale-bone corsets to accentuate their curves. Little Tiger had been wide-eyed the first time she saw an Englishwoman on the street. How odd that these women called themselves "proper ladies" and labelled the Chinese "heathens" when the Englishwomen displayed their breasts like melons on a fruit cart!

It was all so puzzling. Just because they looked different and prayed to a single unseen God instead of revering their ancestors, were they not women just the same? Did they not have the same feelings, the same need to be loved by their parents, their children, and their men?

Ah — their men! The foreigners settling into Hong Kong from many countries — did these men have different desires and hopes than the Chinese men she had met? It was hard to know.

In carefully enunciated English, Little Tiger greeted the missionary lady. "Happy New Year. Have a fantastic shopping day!"

The missionary lady made the sign of the cross to bless her but didn't pull out any money from her pocket. Nevertheless Little Tiger gave a small bow, smiled, and forged into the crowd.

But she stopped dead in her tracks. There, coming toward her, was Mr. Ho and Little Kwong. The boy had sprouted up into a lad in long pants. Little Tiger wanted to hug him and tell him that his small kindnesses had made life bearable for her, but she didn't dare get close enough to be recognized by her former master. She pulled her felt hat farther down her forehead and held a handful of firecrackers in front of her face, hoping they would hide her. But someone jostled her from behind and she stumbled headfirst into Mr. Ho, dropping all her firecrackers on the ground. Mr. Ho reared back and his English bowler hat fell onto the earth right in front of her.

Little Tiger reached down, brushed the dirt off the hat, and handed it back to him, keeping her head down to avoid his eyes. He ran his thumb along the brim, dusted it again with a gloved hand, and placed it carefully on his head. Only then did he look at her.

Little Tiger was now staring directly into Mr. Ho's face. What she saw in his eyes was a dark fury but no flicker of recognition. He apparently saw a young man standing in front of him, not the girl who had once been his *mui jai*.

He spat out the words: "Be careful, you clumsy oaf. This hat is worth ten of you."

Little Tiger bowed from her waist and, with her deepest voice, mumbled a grovelling apology. "Yes, honourable sir, I will be more careful."

With a wave of his hand Mr. Ho dismissed the annoying young man and moved on, but Little Kwong picked up a handful of the firecrackers that she had dropped and handed them back to her. She almost cried in gratitude. He was still a thoughtful boy.

Only when they were far away did Little Tiger allow herself a triumphant smile. She'd fooled the one man who could stand in her way and expose her as an ungrateful and indebted servant. Even the boy hadn't recognized her. Delighted that her disguise worked so well, she felt a surge of pride. She was truly first class. First Class PLUS.

"Get your firecrackers here!" she sang out more loudly.

Trudging through the open square, she noticed a group of men gathered under a new recruiting poster for the Canadian Pacific Railway that was pasted to the wall.

She stared at the painted image in the centre of the poster. A white man with a curled moustache and piercing eyes seemed to look right at her. She had never seen eyes like his before, so clear and blue. He was a rugged man, a North-West Mounted Policeman with a square jaw, wearing a wide-brimmed hat and a scarlet tunic. Underneath his picture, in Chinese and English, a caption read: NICHOL RAILWAY COMPANY. GOOD MEN NEEDED TO BUILD A RAILWAY. EARN ONE DOLLAR EACH DAY. RETURN PASSAGE PAID.

Here was the answer to all of her worries about getting across the ocean! Passage paid. One dollar a day. She could travel to Gold Mountain, find her father, and make her own fortune. She took a long, deep breath and felt something new stirring inside her. She hardly recognized it for what it was: hope.

Hurrying toward the factory, she passed a fortune teller's booth and her heart skipped a beat. Another auspicious omen. There was another white man, this one in person, standing at the booth waving a piece of paper in front of the fortune teller's face. He was tall with handsome features, and dressed in a suit even finer than Mr. Ho's. His eyes were even bluer than the Mountie in the poster. He seemed flustered and pointed to the writing on the paper. "See! An address. Here."

The fortune teller answered in Chinese, telling the *gwailo* that he couldn't read the writing and couldn't understand a word he was saying.

The foreigner raised his voice, as if by speaking louder and gesturing more he would make the man understand his English. "Think! It's vital that I find this address," he shouted.

Little Tiger listened carefully. His voice sounded different from other English speakers she'd known — Little Kwong's teacher, or her tutor, Mr. Relic. Maybe this one wasn't from England like them, maybe he was from the *New* World, like the Mountie. Could he have a connection with the railway company?

The perplexed fortune teller scanned the paper, then pointed to his fortune packets and made his sales pitch in Chinese. "Why don't you buy a fortune message from me? Very good luck."

The white man threw his hands in the air and looked around for someone, anyone, who could understand him. About to offer her help, Little Tiger sized him up. Would his eyes get even more blue like the sea if she came close to him? He seemed desperate and, judging by his appearance, he would probably pay good money to be led through the twisted alleys to his destination. She started toward him, but at that moment, out of the corner of her eye, she saw a squint-eyed bully from her factory sidle up to her stall.

She knew who he was — Di Hong, a thug in training from the factory. Sometimes he would secretly slit the bottom of the boxes that Little Tiger loaded, so that when she lifted them the firecrackers fell to the floor. In the market she'd seen him steal fruit from old ladies too feeble to give chase. She knew this guy was up to no good and must be stopped. But as she was running back to her stall, he lit a match to the fuses of all her firecrackers hanging there. WHIZ! BOOM! BANG! The mass of fireworks exploded. Shoppers dove for cover as the small "snappers" popped and sizzled in a mad frenzy. Raging, Little Tiger shouted to the crowd, "Grab him! He set the fire!"

But her voice was lost in the din as, one after another, the big rockets exploded with a deafening roar. She tried to follow the bully as he raced off, but the crowd was now standing shoulder to shoulder looking upward and she couldn't get through. They cupped their hands over their ears, mesmerized by the rockets whizzing up over their heads, riveted by the sight of a sky exploding into rainbows. Some fireworks took the shape of dragons dancing high in the sky before dissolving into sparkling rivers. There were oohs and aahs and wild clapping. For the crowd, it meant a glorious future. Glorious for everyone but Little Tiger. She fought back tears and balled her fists into tight knots of frustration. It was too much to bear. All that work, for what? Her dreams had just exploded in front of her.

When the smoke died down, she looked around for the foreigner but he had disappeared. No surprise. Nothing was going her way. She cleared the debris around her wreck of a stall and headed off to her job at the factory. Her only consolation was that she still *had* a job, even if the work was tedious and the dust from the black powder they put inside the explosives clung to her clothes and clogged her throat. The only bright spot was learning how to harness the power of black powder under the watchful eye of the ancient master, Mr. Zhou.

Already late, and afraid the boss would dock her pay, Little Tiger zigzagged through the back passages behind the market square and arrived at the dingy factory, out of breath. She quickly started work, lifting a box full of fireworks. CRASH! They fell onto the floor and rolled under the tables. The bottom had been slashed — again! There was a roar of laughter from behind her.

"Loser! Pick them all up!"

It was the bully Di Hong — again. He raised his fist and moved in for a fight, but Little Tiger had had enough. She pulled her knife out of her sleeve and brought it up to his face. Di Hong halted in his tracks, surprised that she had the guts to carry a weapon like that.

At that moment, Mr. Zhou called from the courtyard, "Little Tiger, come here! Time to use your brain, not your hands."

Di Hong turned away and Little Tiger tucked her knife back into her sleeve.

Thank goodness Mr. Zhou had saved her from doing something really dumb and winding up in jail, or dead. She was fond of the ancient master. He was older than most grandfathers. His hair was little more than fine white wisps, his skin was shrunken over sharp bones, but what amazed Little Tiger was that, even though Mr. Zhou was almost blind, he had a sixth sense of what was happening and, relying only on touch, he could perform magic with black powder.

He placed a walnut shell and a box of firecrackers in front of her.

"Can you split this?" he asked. "We can share the nut inside."

Little Tiger looked at the old man as if he had lost his mind. Of course she could! It was a simple task for someone so first class. She took her knife and made a hole in one side of the shell, inserted a tiny firecracker into the hole, struck a match, and lit the fuse. POP! The walnut exploded into a dozen fragments and left only a fine dust on the table. Little Tiger beamed with pride at the Ancient. But to her surprise he was frowning and shaking his head from side to side.

"Look at that," he said, his voice dripping disappointment. "This is worth nothing now. We cannot eat this walnut. You must explode the shell but not destroy what is inside. Try it again. This time, the shell should split and the nut inside remain whole."

Little Tiger looked at him in disbelief. "That's impossible. *You* do it!"

The old man accepted the challenge. He chose another whole walnut, examined the shell from every angle, then selected two even smaller firecrackers. With a sharp knife, he cut two slits on opposite sides of the shell and inserted a firecracker into each one.

"It's not only a case of how much powder you use but where you place the charges that counts. Come — you light one, I'll light the other," he instructed.

Together, Mr. Zhou and Little Tiger each lit one of the tiny firecrackers on opposite sides of the shell. Another POP! and the shell burst apart, leaving two clean halves of the nut. Mr. Zhou popped his half into his mouth and beamed.

"Good to eat. Nice and clean."

Little Tiger stared at her half, wide-eyed and mystified, but full of admiration for the Ancient's skill. Mr. Zhou then took a small red envelope from his pocket and handed it to the kid. It was a fortune message for the New Year. She thanked him, ripped it open and read aloud these words:

YOUR LUCK IS ABOUT TO CHANGE.

Chapter Four

Little Tiger read her good-luck message once more before putting it in her pocket next to the handful of coins she'd been paid for her week's work in the factory. Perhaps her luck *would* change. As the sun dropped behind the mountains surrounding the harbour, she stopped at the laundry to pick up a bundle of clean shirts for her tutor, Mr. Relic, then made her way across town.

The island of Hong Kong was a bustling place. Little Tiger started in the west part of town, where she had lived with the Hos. All the Chinese — labourers to shipping magnates — lived and worked there to be near their temples, shops, and tea houses. Walking from there to the eastern part of town where the foreigners lived was like entering a different world. Gas lamps now lit her way along clean streets lined with flower gardens. She passed the grand British government buildings, the cricket pitch, a museum, post office, and library.

Towering over her was the highest point of the island, Victoria Peak, named after the faraway British queen. That's where the foreign big shots, the *tai-pans,* built their houses and fancy clubs. It was against the law for the Chinese to live with the *gwailo* — the white ghosts — unless, of course, it was as their servants.

She stopped at a ramshackle house on the edge of the foreign enclave, a place where outcasts like Mr. Relic lived. He was one of her laundry customers, a crusty old Brit with rheumy eyes and a bulbous red nose that blossomed even more after each of his alcohol binges. He spent most of his money on gin and rarely had enough to pay Little Tiger for his clean shirts, so he tutored her in English in exchange. She thought it was a fair deal. Building on what she already knew, she figured that reading and speaking English would help her in Gold Mountain. Her favourite word was *fantastic.* She loved to roll that word around her mouth and found a dozen reasons every day to say "FAN-TAS-TIC!"

As she lifted her hand to knock on Mr. Relic's door, she saw a half-dozen pieces of paper pinned to it, all from the Nichol Railway Company. She collected them in one hand and knocked loudly with the other.

"Mr. Relic. Mr. Relic! How are you? I am fantastic."

From within she heard a rustling of sheets and the thump of one heavy foot hitting the floor and, after a pause, another one. Then a fit of coughing. She grimaced at the sounds and pounded even harder on the door. Finally it creaked open and Mr. Relic, draped in a blanket over his rumpled suit, peered at her through bloodshot eyes.

"Dear God … I'm still alive! Come in, my boy."

Relic took the clean shirts and threw them on the sagging bed. She noticed a big bottle of gin on the bedside table. He pointed to a laundry bag in the corner and, speaking Chinese, told Little Tiger to take away the dirty shirts.

"Sir, you promised to speak English," said Little Tiger.

Relic shrugged. "Your English is quite good enough."

"I want it to be more good," she answered.

"Not 'more good' — 'better.' I want it to be bett-er."

Little Tiger squeezed her eyes in concentration and focused on twisting her tongue around the troublesome *T* sounds.

"Bedder."

"BeTT-er," said Relic. "Say TT."

"BeTT-er," repeated Little Tiger.

Mr. Relic nodded with approval. "Good, boy, good!"

Little Tiger handed him the notes she'd collected from the front door, then circled the room picking up his soiled shirts.

"From your office," she explained. "The Nichol Railway Company. Maybe important news from Gold Mountain."

The sad-faced Mr. Relic crumpled the notes into his wastebasket.

Little Tiger wasn't sure exactly what Mr. Relic did at the office. She only saw him in his own place, where mostly he was slumped in bed, still wearing his suit, with damp cloths draped over his eyes. What she did know was that the Nichol Railway Company was in British Columbia and that's where her father had said he was heading.

Relic ignored her as he searched for a match to light his cigar. "You don't need better English, boy, if your only plan is to waste it on Gold Mountain."

"Maybe I find my father there."

Relic shook his head with disgust and Little Tiger felt her cheeks flush in anger.

"What you mean, waste it? I make lots of money there. How much a dollar buy for me?"

"A dollar? Six bottles of wine. Good wine. Two shirts."

"Fantastic!" beamed Little Tiger. "I make money to buy two shirts every day at Gold Mountain."

Relic took a swig from the gin bottle and polished it off. Little Tiger proudly pulled out her fortune paper.

"See what that say — my luck is about to change!"

Relic frowned at her. "Luck can change in two directions. Do you want to end up like your father?"

Her face fell. "Sir, we do not know if he dead or alive. I go find myself."

Suddenly there was a loud knock on the door. Relic signalled Little Tiger not to speak as a voice called out, "Mr. Relic! Are you in there? It's me, James Nichol."

Relic looked at Little Tiger in panic. He mimed fainting and pushed Little Tiger toward the door. Reluctantly, she opened the small portal to look out on to the street. To her amazement she found herself looking into the blue, blue eyes of the handsome foreigner from the market.

So his name was James Nichol! In a flash she realized that her luck had indeed changed. With a name like that, he must be connected to the Nichol Railway Company. Perhaps he could hire her. She could barely speak. Stuttering, she managed "Mr. Relic very sick."

"Thank goodness!" said the foreigner, "At last someone who speaks English."

Little Tiger grinned. "I speak it beTT-er."

The man waved a white envelope and tried to peer past Little Tiger into the room. He raised his voice so that Relic could hear him.

"Is he too sick to pick up his final *payment*?"

At that word, Relic, on high alert, called out, "Payment?"

Little Tiger repeated "Mr. Relic very, very sick," and snapped the portal shut. James gave the door a kick and yelled, "Is he *dead?* Because if he isn't, my father wants to know why he hasn't put two thousand damn Chinamen on a boat to British Columbia."

Little Tiger slapped her forehead. Ah! So Mr. Relic was a recruiter for the Nichol Company and needed more men, yet he wouldn't hire her to work on the railway. For a moment she was furious with him, then realized that here was an opportunity staring her in the face: Mr. Relic didn't want her to go to Gold Mountain but this Mr. Nichol might. She just had to prove herself. She pushed open the door and came out onto the street where James stood slapping the envelope against his thigh in frustration.

"Hi! Hi! Mr. James Nichol!"

She stared at his fine clothes and shiny leather boots. He was even more impressive than the Mountie on the poster. He was tall and handsome, but younger, and he didn't have a moustache. She threw back her shoulders and stuck out her chin.

"You need workers? I will work for you, Mr. James. My name is Xiao Hu. It means Little Tiger."

James smiled at the kid's nickname and his bravado. "We need men, not boys ..."

"I am eighteen years old. I read. I write. I speak English FANTASTIC!"

"Yeah, you lie too. You're fifteen at most and you're a runt. More kitty cat than tiger."

"I do not lie," protested Little Tiger. "I can do many things. I am fantastic with black powder!"

James smirked and patted the boy on the shoulder. "Sure, kid. Maybe someday."

He turned to walk away. Just then Relic, looking almost presentable in his suit jacket and panama hat, came out onto the street and extended his hand to James in a formal greeting.

"Good day, young man. Please accept my apology for my recent indisposition. A recurring malady common in the tropics."

James sniffed the alcohol on the old man's breath. "Yes," he said, "I can smell it."

Relic reached for his pay envelope but James pulled it back. "My father wants to know why we're short the last hundred men."

Relic looked James in the eye. "My dear boy, between myself and the other fine recruiters on this fair isle, we have assembled one thousand and nine hundred men, a goodly number."

"No. You promised my father that *two thousand* men would be on the boats to Canada. He's sent me here to make sure that happens."

Little Tiger's eyes opened wide. This was the best luck! Mr. James not only did important work for the Nichol Railway, he was the son of the owner. He needed a hundred more recruits, and he saw through Mr. Relic's excuses.

Relic went on and on about how difficult it was to find good men and how he required a monthly stipend to find the last of the recruits, but James was adamant that he wouldn't see another cent until the last one hundred men, able and ready to head overseas, showed up at the office. With that, he walked away.

Little Tiger admired the gumption of the stern-faced James and followed him, starry-eyed, until he rounded the corner, hailed a rickshaw, and drove off. Relic came up beside her as she said to herself, "For sure I will go to Gold Mountain now!"

He sadly shook his head. "Oh dear, oh dear, oh dear. Be careful what you wish for, boy. You might just bloody well get it."

***

Back in her room that night, Little Tiger lit a kerosene lamp and bowed with joss sticks at her family altar. Amid the bits of fruit and smoldering incense was the family photograph, taken so long ago, that her mother had given her as she lay dying. Little Tiger picked it up and touched it lovingly.

"I am coming, *Baba*," she whispered. "I will keep my promise, *Ama*."

She removed the hat she wore constantly as part of her disguise. Over the years she'd stopped shaving the front of her head because it was never seen, but she still kept the long braid down her back. She undid it now and brushed her hair to keep it shiny, then removed her long jacket and, with a sigh of relief, unwound the cloth that bound her breasts so tightly. She took her fortune paper out of her trouser pocket, slipped out of her baggy pants, and pulled a nightshirt over her slender body. As she put her head on her pillow, she read the fortune paper one more time. *Your luck is about to change.*

Indeed it was — thanks to Mr. James Nichol, son of the railway boss. Yes, he'd turned her down this time, but she would prove her skills to him, how fantastic she was with black powder, how useful she would be on an explosives crew, and he would surely hire her.

The next day, Little Tiger showed up at the Nichol Railway Company office. She was flabbergasted by what she saw: there stood a ragged mob of emaciated, vacant-eyed men that Mr. Relic had assembled and James, standing beside his translator Wang Yi, was surveying them with distaste.

He snarled at Mr. Relic. "With just days to go, you expect me to take these wharf rats and opium smokers? I see better men on the street every day. Send them away."

Wang Yi told the crowd that the boss wouldn't take them. Little Tiger watched with growing unease as the mob of scrawny men realized they'd been dragged there for nothing. No wonder they were angry. Relic must have made big promises of money for showing up at the office, plus riches awaiting them in Gold Mountain. The crowd grumbled and the leader motioned the men to surge forward ... to attack James! But he was ready. He quickly tugged a gun from a holster on his hip and fired a shot into the air. Little Tiger was surprised. The crowd recoiled and muttered curses, then shuffled away.

Relic didn't seem to care but Little Tiger saw another opportunity to be hired. If *she* found the last one hundred men, surely Mr. James would hire her.

"Mr. James," she called out, "I find you strong workers, at my factory. I tell them about big money from the Nichol Railway Company."

James turned to Relic. "See that? Even this kid knows where to find men."

Little Tiger's heart beat faster.

***

At lunch the factory workers sat on long benches, slumped over their noodle bowls. Little Tiger scurried from one to another, whispering that she could get them to Gold Mountain and its riches.

There was sound of a commotion outside the factory. Even before she saw them, Little Tiger recognized the voices of Mr. James, Mr. Relic, and Wang Yi. James was standing at the doorway, obviously confused by an elderly man trying to tell him something.

"What's this man jabbering about?" he asked.

Wang Yi bowed to the old man and whispered to James, "This gentleman is asking you to remove your footwear before entering."

James refused. To Little Tiger he looked as if he rarely took orders from anyone, especially a translator. She wondered if she should intervene and was happy when Mr. Relic did.

"Take off your boots, for Christ's sake!" he ordered. "They're too dangerous around explosives. One spark and we'd all be done for."

Shocked, James looked from Relic to the translator and the old worker at the door, then struggled out of his boots. He had a lot to learn.

Next he barged into the lunchroom, calling out to the workers, "You there! You men! How would you like to make some real money?"

There were blank faces in front of him so he turned to the translator. "Go on. Tell them what I'm saying."

Relic looked worried and muttered, "Oh dear, oh dear, oh dear."

Reluctantly, Wang Yi translated. He told the men that his boss wanted to offer them a better job, then repeated exactly what Little Tiger had already whispered to them at the lunch tables.

"One dollar a day for building a railway." He smiled.

Little Tiger heard footsteps and turned to look behind her. There stood the factory supervisor, his hands on his hips, glaring at James and Wang Yi.

"Shut your mouth," he said in Chinese. "Keep your hands off my workers!"

Wang Yi looked afraid but James, not understanding, shouted loudly, "In one year you can make over three hundred dollars!"

Suddenly a worker raised his head and motioned toward the entrance door. The room became deathly quiet. Even James stopped talking. Straddling the opening was an immense man holding a walking stick, dressed in traditional Chinese clothing with a rounded pillbox cap on his head, but a British camelhair coat slung over his shoulders. It was Lei Mo, who ran the most powerful and violent gang in Hong Kong. Behind him stood a smug Di Hong, the factory bully who'd blown up Little Tiger's stall, plus three stocky men with their arms crossed.

Everyone feared this big boss man, Lei Mo. The factory supervisor kowtowed before him and discreetly handed him a thick envelope. Little Tiger knew it was a bribe for "protection" of the factory. Protection was a big joke. The only thing Lei Mo protected was his own power and money grabbing, but crossing him meant death.

Relic blanched at the sight of Lei Mo. The translator was petrified and lifted his hands in apology. Little Tiger, hopping up from her bench, grabbed hold of James's sleeve, and tried to tug him toward the back door.

"Time to go far away!" she whispered to him, but James refused to budge.

Di Hong said something to the gang lord and pointed a finger at Little Tiger. Lei Mo stared at her, then put his hand around the translator's throat.

"You have no business here!" he growled, glaring at Relic, James, and Little Tiger.

To Little Tiger's dismay, James didn't seem to realize the danger they were in. He whispered to Relic, "Who's this guy with the teapot hat?"

Relic smiled nervously and answered through gritted teeth, "You have chosen a factory under the protection of the local gang lord, Lei Mo."

The gang lord shifted his walking stick ominously from one hand to the other. James was reaching his hand into his coat to take out his gun, but Relic snarled, "Don't be a fool, you'll blow us to kingdom come!" He pointed to the explosives stacked along every wall of the factory. James's eyes widened and he quickly pulled his hand back. Relic bowed to Lei Mo and, in his best Chinese, said, "My apologies, sir. We'll be on our way now. Good day."

He grabbed James by the arm and they backed out the door. Lei Mo lifted his walking stick triumphantly and signalled the factory supervisor to follow him into the back room.

As soon as they left, Little Tiger ran outside and called, "Mr. James, wait!"

James looked at the kid scrambling after him. "You again! What is it this time?"

"To build the iron road you use black powder, right?" asked Little Tiger.

"Explosives. Of course."

"I can do black powder. I explode really fantastic."

James laughed. "You'd explode, all right."

"Hire me!" she insisted. "I read, I write, I will be big help. I can bring men from the factory."

Relic looked at her, appalled. "That's bloody lunacy, my boy. Lei Mo will slit you from the belly to the chops."

Little Tiger stood her ground. "I'm not afraid of Lei Mo."

James considered her offer. "All right, kid. I'll pay you a shilling for every good man you bring to the square in front of the office by eight o'clock tonight."

Relic threw up his arms in disgust. "Fools. Both of you!"

Little Tiger scurried back to the factory, and when Lei Mo had left she quietly began to recruit again, whispering in the ear of each worker. When she walked past Di Hong, her heart gave a little thump and she said nothing. He snarled at her and flashed a shiny knife tucked up his own sleeve.

"One day you'll wish you never threatened me," he said. "One day I'll be as big as Lei Mo is."

Little Tiger couldn't resist laughing at him. "You're almost that fat now!" she said.

If the supervisor hadn't walked by at that exact moment … well, Little Tiger didn't even want to think about what Di Hong might have done to her. Besides, there were more important things on her mind, like her promise to bring ninety-nine recruits to the square that night so she would be hired as the hundredth.

At eight o'clock Relic and James were waiting in the courtyard behind the railway company's offices. Proudly Little Tiger strode in, leading a string of workers from her factory.

"Here we are. Ninety-nine men, and me. All ready to get on ship to go to Gold Mountain."

James liked what he saw — these were sturdy men — and he handed the kid an envelope full of shillings. But she had a bigger goal: to secure her own place on the crew. She pulled a couple of sticks of dynamite from her pocket.

"We all sign with you for Gold Mountain, but first you watch how I do black powder."

James laughed. "Take the money and beat it, kid. You're too puny."

Just as she prepared to show off her dynamite skills, Little Tiger heard a shuffling noise behind her. It was Lei Mo and his thugs emerging from the shadows. Di Hong was with them and when Little Tiger met his eyes, his face twisted into a triumphant smirk. She looked down and saw that they were all carrying machetes.

"Nobody steals workers from one of my factories," growled Lei Mo, advancing on Relic and James.

"Oh, shit!" yelled Relic, and ran off down an alley.

Terrified, all of Little Tiger's recruits followed fast behind him.

She shouted at them, "Come back, you cowards!" but they disappeared into the night.

James pulled out his gun, pointed it at Lei Mo, and turned to Little Tiger. "Tell them to drop their knives."

Little Tiger screamed at them in Chinese, "Drop your knives or he'll feed his bullets into your skulls and turn them to mush."

She looked back at James. He was holding his gun as steady as he could but he was sweating and blinking hard. She realized he had probably never fired a gun at anyone before.

Di Hong slid up beside Lei Mo. "Look! The guy's hand is shaking. He's too scared to shoot."

Seeing this, Lei Mo signalled one of his henchmen to sneak up on James around the side. Then he spat on the ground and growled at Little Tiger. "So you're the little shit who joined this pair! You should have thought first before helping them steal my workers."

At that moment, the henchman came up behind James and hit him on the head with the handle of his machete. James cried out and lost his balance … and his gun. It fell to the ground and Lei Mo lunged forward to grab it, but Little Tiger stomped hard on his hand and scooped up the gun. Lei Mo fell back, screaming in pain, "Goddamn, you. You've broken my hand!"

Triumphantly Little Tiger tossed the gun back to James, who by now had righted himself. He held the gun as steady as he could and pointed it at the gang.

Little Tiger grinned at them. "Eat this!" she cried, lighting a dynamite stick and throwing it right at them.

Lei Mo, cringing with pain, looked on in horror as the stick of dynamite dropped in front of him, its short fuse already hissing. Di Hong cowered behind his boss and grabbed on to him as a shield. Lei Mo struggled to get away, but with his wounded hand and the bully clinging to his back he was like a crippled crab. The dynamite sizzled.

"Get off me, you snivelling coward," screamed Lei Mo, trying to shake him off. But Di Hong only tightened his grip and watched in horror as a stream of hot pee ran down his leg and pooled at his boss's feet.

"You're dead, Di Hong. Dead!" spat Lei Mo. He lurched sideways, then tripped and fell flat on his backside.

Little Tiger laughed, but James was shocked and shouted, "We're going to get killed when that thing blows up!"

"I told you I was fantastic with black powder," said Little Tiger. "Watch."

The dynamite fuse burned into the stick, but there was only a feeble pop.

"It's fake!" laughed Little Tiger. "Now we run to Mr. Relic."

With Lei Mo's gang in pursuit, the two of them careened through the market, toppling everything in their path. When they reached Relic's door, Little Tiger pounded on it frantically, shouting that it was them. Armed with a gun himself, Relic opened the door and pulled them inside. By the time Lei Mo and his men found Relic's place, all three of them — Little Tiger, Relic, and James — were hidden under the floor boards. They held their breath as the gang searched every corner of Relic's rooms, walking right across the boards over their heads, and found nothing.

"They'll all pay for this," threatened Lei Mo as he led his goons out the door.

The threesome under the floor boards waited until all was clear and heaved a collective sigh of relief. Little Tiger gazed up at the handsome Mr. James beside her and he smiled back.

Then her eyes lit up. "Wait! I know the most fantastic place to get workers. I promise."

Relic raised his eyebrow and sighed. "Oh dear, oh dear, oh dear!"

CHAPTER FIVE

The oarsman stood in the back of the low-lying boat as he paddled his three passengers up to Little Tiger's home village. It was desolate. The kid pointed to a simple cottage on the banks of the river. "There — my home till twelve years old."

Relic leaned back in the boat against bags of rice and lit his cigar.

"Wherever we are, at least it puts a distance between us and that monster Lei Mo."

James shuddered and asked Little Tiger why she was so sure they could find men in this village who would go to Canada on such short notice.

"Brave men here," she replied. "Like my father. They fighted the Manchu army."

Relic corrected her grammar. "Fought. Fought. Fought."

"Ah, yes. He *fought* them until he go to Gold

Mountain. Mr. James, let me come to Gold Mountain, please! Didn't I save your life?"

James turned and looked at the kid in astonishment. Had he forgotten that it was he who had enraged Lei Mo by bringing workers from the factory? That he had defied the gang lord and stomped on his hand in the fight? "Saved my life? Sure you did, after you almost got us both slaughtered."

"I got your gun for you," protested Little Tiger. "Now I get men you need and go to Gold Mountain with them."

"Kid, find the men and I'll pay you, but I told you, you're not going to Gold Mountain."

How could she convince him that she would be fantastic on the railway crew? Mr. Zhou had told her that black powder was the only way to blast through rock to prepare a railway track. Surely if she found these last one hundred men in her village *and* showed James her skill with dynamite, he wouldn't have any choice but to take her along. She would be his Number One boy.

The oarsman brought the boat to a stop at the wharf and they got off. As they walked into the destitute village, Little Tiger turned to James. "I teach you important Chinese words now. For 'a dollar a day,' say '*yat mun yatyat*,' and for 'Gold Mountain' — that is easy — '*gum san*.'"

Valiantly, James tried to pronounce the words. Little Tiger nearly doubled over laughing.

"What's so funny?" asked James.

"You just said, 'I am in love with a donkey.'" She giggled.

His face fell.

"Come on, James, give it a go," insisted Relic.

James tried again with a different emphasis.

Little Tiger grimaced. "BeTT-er," she said and flashed her white teeth in a wide smile.

"What a shame a beautiful smile like that is wasted on a boy," Relic said with a sigh.

Little Tiger ignored him, bouncing with excitement as she pointed to the crowd of men gathering in the square. James marched toward them with Relic and Little Tiger close behind.

"You talk to them, kid," he told her. "Tell them what I say. We'll get these men on the other side of the ocean and show my father I can do it — bring two thousand workers to build his goddamn railway for him. Then I can get back to my *real* life: wine, women, and hockey."

Little Tiger took all of this in.

Soon, the trio stood in front of the villagers in the mud square. Little Tiger thought she recognized two boys she'd grown up with, Wang Ma and Cheung Wei. Yes, it was them — now grown men, standing at the front with their arms crossed — muscular arms and stocky thighs from heavy work in the fields. Proudly she pointed them out to James. "See, not puny men here."

He nodded and instructed her to translate his pitch exactly.

"We're hiring men for Gold Mountain! One dollar a day!" she called out.

The villagers crowded closer and she continued her impassioned plea. "For your family you could make three hundred dollars in one year!"

But the men seemed suspicious. It sounded too good to be true.

Little Tiger persisted. "What do you have here? Nothing. Do you want to die here? Why don't you take a chance?"

The men turned to each other, debating loudly. Wang Ma asked about the gold. He'd heard it was lying in ditches, ready for the taking. Relic looked skeptical but James nodded to Little Tiger. This was her cue.

"Mr. James promises that any gold you find, you can keep for yourself."

There was a holler of approval and backslapping among the men.

Little Tiger shouted enthusiastically, "Now tell all your neighbours that we're set to go."

Wang Ma turned to his friend Chung Wei and smiled as if he'd just won a pile of money at mah-jong. "I'll go!" he cried.

Other men eagerly followed his lead. Relic signed them up, telling them to say goodbye to their families and show up at Dock 10 of the Hong Kong harbour in exactly two days' time.

Now the three of them could head back. The oarsman deposited them downriver at a little riverside restaurant to wait for the last leg to Hong Kong. They congratulated each other on finding the last of the men as Little Tiger slurped a bowl of noodles, James sipped tea, and Relic smoked yet another cigar. On the other side of the narrow river three teenage girls shyly looked across at James, then giggled and whispered to one another. Little Tiger couldn't help but notice how James's eyes twinkled as he smiled back at them.

Relic noticed too. "Look, but never touch, Mr. Nichol. That way heartache lies."

Little Tiger didn't understand what Relic meant. She knew that Englishmen paid money to dance and drink with Chinese girls and to lie with them afterward, but she had never known of an Englishman and a Chinese girl actually falling in love and living together as a couple.

James peered at Relic. "You sound like a sadder but wiser man," he said.

Little Tiger listened carefully for Relic's answer.

"Wiser? I don't know. I did have a Chinese almost-wife for a time, in Singapore. But her family despised me. And the company for which I worked took a very dim view. So I had to send the lovely little thing packing."

Ah! That was one of the secrets from Mr. Relic's past. Little Tiger wondered if he had loved his almost-wife. Did he send her away because her family disapproved or because he would lose his job? She didn't know what to think. She'd never known of a Chinese girl married to a foreigner but now she could understand the possibility. She found Mr. James very attractive — for a *gwailo*. And that feeling surprised her. Living as a boy, she had suppressed any attraction to men, but this man was a puzzling mix of arrogance and charm. If her parents were still alive, if she was still a girl, she would have been engaged by now to a Chinese boy approved by them. That was the way it was. That was the way it had always been. But she wondered if that was the way it would always be.

All the way home on the boat she thought about it. When they reached Hong Kong, James hailed a rickshaw and said goodnight to Relic and Little Tiger.

Relic warned him, "Be sure to go straight to your hotel, young man. Lei Mo will have his thugs out looking for you."

"First I have to send a message to my father," said James.

"But the New Year's celebrations are starting," said Relic, pointing at the first firecracker lighting up the sky to herald the New Year. "Everything will be closed."

Little Tiger butted in. "Tell your father how I found the men."

James smiled at her. "I appreciate all you've done, Little Tiger, but I want to prove to my father that I have done the job he sent me to do, contrary to all his expectations."

Relic became thoughtful. "It's the way of fathers and sons, young man. Sons try to please their fathers and it is never good enough, until one day the son surpasses the father."

"Some fathers are never satisfied," muttered James.

"And some fathers not there at all," sighed Little Tiger.

Relic put his hand on her shoulder and gave it a squeeze.

"This is what I will write in the telegram," said James. "Good News. Stop. Two thousand healthy and hale crew ready to sail. Stop. Happy Chinese New Year. Stop."

"Why stop?" asked Little Tiger, puzzled.

Relic answered. "My boy, James will send a message over telegraph wires — a miracle of communication. But messages sent this way are easily garbled and misunderstood. Saying 'stop' shows that it is the end of a sentence."

She leaped at the opportunity.

"Mr. James, you should telegraph 'Little Tiger is coming. STOP. Little Tiger is fantastic with black powder. STOP.'"

James patted her on the head and laughed as he climbed into his rickshaw.

Relic called to him, "Watch out for Lei Mo. He wants to get revenge on us."

But James had already sped off.

Relic bent down to say goodbye to Little Tiger. With tenderness and deep concern, he looked her in the eye. "Make sure you find a safe bed tonight, Little Tiger," he told her, and strolled off down the long street, festooned with lanterns for the New Year celebrations.

Back in her tiny room, Little Tiger had things to do. She set up her altar and prayed to her ancestors that the village recruits would show up as they had promised. She held the photograph of her family close to her and caressed the image of her father.

"I will find you," she whispered.

Then she packed the tintype and what little else she owned into her rucksack. Yes, she would make one last try to be on that boat to Gold Mountain in the morning. She tried to sleep but she only tossed and turned, listening to the gongs announcing the dragon dancers and the sound of thousands of fireworks exploding to signal the arrival of the Year of the Horse. Would this be the year when her luck would change?

***

Two days later, on the dock, Little Tiger counted the men who'd come from the village. *Yes!* she said to herself, relieved that they had all kept their promise. When James arrived she boasted, "Ninety-nine men plus me — one hundred!"

James smiled indulgently and pulled out his money clip. He was a man of his word and he would pay her for recruiting these men. He peeled off the notes and handed them to her.

"Now where's Relic?" he asked. "He said he'd be at the office, but … ha, ha! He's probably in a drunken stupor now that the job is done. However, I promised to pay him and I will."

As James headed to the office, the ship hands started to line up all the Chinese men waiting on the dock. Little Tiger trotted behind him. She didn't know what to think, what to do, how to react. Was it possible that James would leave her behind after all she had done to help him? In desperation she tugged on his arm and pressed some of the money into his hand. "See. I pay myself for the ocean passage."

He looked down at her. "Long life, happiness, and prosperity to you. You've got a lot of spunk, little buddy. I really mean that, but I told you — you're not coming. You're too small."

Still she traipsed after him calling out, "Please, Mr. James, please take me to Gold Mountain."

They reached the Nichol Company office and James pulled open the door. What they saw inside made them freeze in shock.

"Oh, Jesus!" he cried, clapping his hand over his mouth.

There, slumped in the chair behind the desk, was Relic's body. His throat had been slit and the blood was still oozing from his neck, turning his white shirt a dark crimson. Little Tiger had never seen such a brutal death. She felt as if a knife had cut at her own heart and tears welled up in her eyes. She collapsed in a heap, sobbing.

"Oh dear, oh dear, oh dear," she said, holding her knees and rocking back and forth. "Mr. Relic, you were my only friend."

James put his hand firmly on her shoulder to comfort her. Then he called the police, who asked him a lot of questions while Little Tiger sat in the hall, alone with her grief. The world had utterly changed. Now she was truly alone.

James came to find her and together they watched the uniformed policemen carry Relic's body away on a stretcher. She turned to James. "Only one person could do this."

"I know," he said. "It must be Lei Mo, and I'll bet you're next on his list. Come on, kid, you're coming with me."

"To Gold Mountain?"

James nodded. In her heart, Little Tiger was both ecstatic and terribly sad. This was what she had longed for but it had happened for the wrong reason. Mr. Relic, her friend, was dead.

***

With all three ships ready to board, Little Tiger joined the stream of workers on the Hong Kong dock, two thousand men, four abreast in a line that seemed to stretch forever. As she shuffled up the gangplank, shoulder to shoulder with all these strangers, she realized that she had no idea what lay ahead.

At the top, she turned and searched for James. Ah — there he was, standing with harbour officials reviewing the paperwork for his human cargo. Hoping she could catch his eye, she lingered on the gangplank until a sailor pushed her forward. "Hurry up! Move it! Let's go!"

***

They had been sailing for close to two months and many of the workers had become sick with dysentery, stuck in the dark, dank hold of the schooner. Many had stopped eating because they couldn't keep their food down. Little Tiger wouldn't call it food — slop, more likely. The stench in the hold was overpowering and what little gruel and water they were given came down in a bucket on a rope through a hatch that was only opened twice a day.

Little Tiger longed to feel land under her feet and breathe fresh air. She'd been crammed in the hold ever since leaving Hong Kong, shoulder to shoulder with so many men as the ocean heaved beneath them. Most of them were strangers, a few were from her village, and who was that in the corner? Little Tiger thought she recognized him — yes, it was Di Hong, the bully she'd outsmarted with fake dynamite, trying to hide with his arms locked around his knees. There was nowhere safe for him; not Hong Kong where Lei Mo had put a price on his head, not here on the ship where so many men had been victims of his brutal gang. They were his enemies and would seek revenge. Little Tiger looked him in the eye and he turned away, embarrassed.

The hold was a stinking nightmare, but at least she had one friend — Wang Ma, from her village. He crouched beside her as the hatch opened and light streamed into their prison. Little Tiger took out her photo and, turning away from him, examined it in the unaccustomed light.

"Those your parents?" asked Wang Ma. "They know you're going to Gold Mountain?"

"They're dead," she answered. She didn't confide to him that deep in her heart she clung to the hope that her father was still alive. No, she would only confess that to someone she knew very well.

Wang Ma nodded in sympathy. "When I left, my mother cried her eyes out. I told her that in a year of two, I'll be back to buy her a little farm. Then I'll find myself a wife, maybe two, and we'll have a dozen children."

Little Tiger was unimpressed. "That's your dream? A pair of fat wives and a litter of kids? Me, I want to build a factory in my village so every man can work."

"Just one factory?" Wang Ma teased.

"To start with," said Little Tiger. "Then more, when the farms are replanted."

"You've got big dreams," he said, laughing aloud.

Little Tiger punched him playfully in the chest. "You dream little, you live little," she replied as she wrapped up her precious photo and put it back in her rucksack.

The hatch opened wider and sun streamed into the hold. Little Tiger and Wang Ma shielded their eyes from the sudden brightness. A rope ladder was thrown down.

"Time to get some air," called a sailor from above.

All the men were startled and shouted with joy. Little Tiger was one of the first to scramble up the ladder and onto the deck. She looked out across the railing to the sea. Never had she seen so much water. It stretched up to the sky and around on every side. As she stared out at the horizon, she lost her footing, slipped on the wet wood, and slid across the deck. Right into James himself as he walked with the first mate.

He grabbed her. "Careful, boy, you don't have your sea legs! … Oh, it's *you*, Little Tiger. What a surprise. How are you?"

Little Tiger was amazed, and embarrassed as she tried to stand up. She knew she smelled and her hair was a rat's nest under her hat. There was no way for her to bathe down in the hold, just a bucket and soap occasionally lowered through the hatch that all the workers had to share. There was no privacy down there and she was afraid to undress or unbind herself for fear that one of the men might see that she was a woman. She couldn't take any chances, not now when she was so close to her goal. Besides, the rest of the men in the hold smelled just as bad so she'd been unaware of her own stench … until now. She looked away.

"I smell bad," she muttered.

"A little ripe," he answered gamely. "And you're even more puny. You've lost a lot of weight. By golly, I didn't know things were so bad down below. I'm going to make sure that you all get more food and water, and come up on deck more often."

"Thank you, Mr. James. You are not like the others."

James looked at the slip of a boy in front of him. "Are you still sure this is what you want? Gold Mountain?"

"A dollar a day? And all the gold I find?" she answered. "Oh, yes!"

"It may be harder than anything you've ever done."

"I am hard worker. We all hard workers," said Little Tiger, "but I never build a railway. Mr. James, what *is* a railway?"

James was stunned by the question. "Ah, of course!" he said. "You've never seen a train or a railway. Not in

Hong Kong or Guangdong. And still, you were willing to come?"

Little Tiger nodded. She had her own reasons. James motioned for her to sit beside him on the deck.

"Let me try to explain, kid. A railway is two things: trains and rails. Trains are like huge carts with many wheels. They pull railway cars along the rails. Some of the cars carry animals and supplies and some cars are like little houses."

Little Tiger was confused. "Houses on wheels?" she asked.

"Well, yeah. Oh dear. I'm not doing a good job at this." James ran both of his hands through his hair. "Uh, they're pulled by …"

"Horses?" suggested Little Tiger.

"Well, sort of. Iron horses that snort steam."

Little Tiger wasn't sure she was ready for these strange things in the new world.

"Now, rails," continued James, "are special roads just for trains. First we make a flat, narrow bed of crushed stone, then we lay thick beams of wood, we call them 'ties,' all the same size, this close together." James held his arms about a foot apart. "Then we take two long pieces of iron that have been smoothed on the edges and hammer them into the ties with metal spikes. The train rolls along these pieces of iron."

Little Tiger struggled to imagine iron horses snorting steam, pulling houses on wheels along an iron road.

"Why do you want this iron road?" she asked.

"Canada's a new country," he said, his eyes lighting up. "If we want to grow, we need ways to move people and things from one end of the country to the other. Trains are the fastest way."

"This would be a good thing for China too," said Little Tiger.

"It won't be long," he answered. "In fact, I'm surprised that the Chinese didn't invent the railway. You invented so many other things."

Little Tiger had never heard a white man talk about her countrymen with admiration. Every foreigner she'd met claimed to be superior at everything.

"I've been reading," said James, smiling. "When I wasn't trying to point a gun, or being chased by gangs or saved by street urchins." He poked her in the ribs.

Little Tiger laughed.

James continued his history lesson. "The Chinese invented lots of things — tea, and paper, and printing, and the compass. We would be lost in this ocean without the compass, don't you think? And gunpowder, which led to dynamite and fireworks. You know all about that, don't you, kid?"

Little Tiger beamed. "That why you need many Chinese to build your railway. We are fantastic with black powder … especially me."

A dark cloud seemed to descend on James.

"What's wrong?" she asked.

"The fact is that we want all you Chinese labourers because you work harder for less money than whites, and nobody gives a damn if you die on the job."

"But *you* give a damn, don't you?" asked Little Tiger.

James put his arm around his buddy's shoulder. "You be careful. Promise?"

Little Tiger felt a jolt of electricity at his touch. She had a lot to learn about the railway and the new country of Canada. But she had even more to learn about Mr. James.

Chapter Six

Rain was pelting down when the ship docked in Victoria Harbour, British Columbia. By now it was spring, and Little Tiger was filthy and exhausted after all those months in the hold. She opened her arms to the sky and let the fresh rain run over her face and down her neck. She took a deep breath and thanked her ancestors for bringing her safely to this new world, but her first steps were wobbly after so many weeks on the rolling schooner. She held tight to the railing on her way down the gangplank.

The buildings surrounding the pier were impressive and a lot like the Englishmen's buildings in the other Victoria Harbour, the one she knew in Hong Kong, an ocean and a lifetime away. But on this pier there were only *gwailo*. She looked into their faces, expecting to see welcome smiles, but instead she was met with angry scowls. Well-dressed men, women, and even children shouted and waved their fists at her and her exhausted friends.

"Go home, Chinamen! Filthy scabs, stealing jobs from our men. You're only good for taking out slop pails."

Little Tiger and the other Chinese workers were confused. Most of them couldn't understand the insults being hurled at them in English, but they knew an ugly crowd when they saw one and it was clear that they were not welcome in Canada. But hadn't the Mountie on the poster invited them to this country? Didn't Mr. James beg them to leave their country and their families to work on the railway? Here before her was the harsh reality that Mr. Relic had tried to warn her about: no one wanted her in Canada and life was going to be very hard.

A crush of workers pushed Little Tiger toward the immigration shed. There she lined up with hundreds of others to get their papers stamped by the officials. As she waited, she looked around, hoping to see James. It had been a long time since their talk on the schooner's deck, and while she continued her journey in the stinking hold, he had travelled in luxury in his cabin above. Now that they had landed, where was he? Was he with the immigration officials? Yes, there he was, conferring with them. But who was that running toward him? A beautiful woman with a pile of golden curls, dressed in pink taffeta with a low-cut bodice, threw her arms around him. Little Tiger watched in dismay as he embraced this bundle of pink fluff.

"James Nichol, what an impressive sight!" squealed the woman.

James seemed surprised but delighted. "Melanie! You are a vision," he said.

Melanie pretended to accept the compliment bashfully, but to Little's Tiger's eye this pink fluff was no shy wall-flower. She was a woman on a mission to capture James's heart. "I venture to say your father will be very impressed when he sees all these Chinamen," she said.

James said he'd soon find out. Once their papers were processed, he was going to take his Chinese workers up-river to Hell's Gate, where his father was supervising the most dangerous part of the railway construction.

"Don't tell me you're leaving me here all by my lone-some," cooed the woman in pink, batting her eyelashes.

Little Tiger wanted to gag. She knew a phony when she saw one. A sugary phony at that.

"I have to get my men safely to the jobsite," said James. Then, seeing her smile fade, he added, "They've had a rough journey and deserve a good meal. So I *will* stay to have lunch with you."

"That's better," said Melanie, clapping her hands like a child. "I was afraid you were turning into some-one I didn't know."

She cupped his chin in her hand. "Hmm, there *is* something different, about you. I've never heard so much concern for underlings before, especially for these, uh, what do they call them…? Slant eyes?"

James was taken aback. "It's a hard life in China, Mel. Sure, they're different from us, but these are hardworking men trying to make a living to support their folks back home. And …" he smiled, "they have names for us too, y' know — 'white ghosts,' and 'round eyes.'" Playfully he sniffed her neck. "And they think we smell funny too."

Melanie pretended to hit him with her fan as she leaned into him. "I do not smell. I am scented with the finest French perfume. You like?"

She turned to survey the long line of Chinese men at the immigration desk. "Who are they to insult us with words like that? I'll be glad when they finish our railway and get back to where they belong."

James ignored Melanie's comments and Little Tiger was glad that most of the men couldn't understand this vile woman's words. They'd already given up so much; at least they could keep their dignity.

Melanie linked her arm through James's and headed out the door with him. Little Tiger wished that this lady in pink would go back to where *she* came from and leave James alone. He deserved someone better.

Even though they couldn't read Chinese, the immigration officials scrutinized each document that the workers presented. When Little Tiger stepped up to the desk, she broke into a cold sweat. What if this official turned her away? What if he saw that she wasn't a man? What if he questioned her credentials? She wanted to show that she would be a good worker in Canada and that she was fantastic in English so she smiled and, pronouncing each word very carefully, said, "Hello, sir. My name is *Xiao Hu*. How do you do?"

Hearing the rhyme, the officer raised an eyebrow and nudged the guy beside him. "Whad'ya know? A Chink who thinks he's a regular Shakespeare."

He stamped Little Tiger's papers with the date and wrote her name in his book.

"Good luck, kid," he said. "You'll need it."

Little Tiger wondered if her father might be listed in a book like this one. Surely the Chinese workers who had travelled north from San Francisco had been registered in British Columbia. Maybe she could find a way to check the books to see if her father had made the journey safely and been admitted by these same immigration officials.

***

The workers gathered on the platform, waiting for the train to take them to Hell's Gate. It was true that James had *described* a train, but nothing had prepared Little Tiger for the massive hulk of metal that arrived, belching clouds of steam from its stack and pulling railcars with equipment, supplies, timber, even horses. At this sight, some of the Chinese workers screamed in terror, thinking it must have come from the spirit world. But they soon realized that this iron horse was very real. Within minutes they were jammed into open flat cars with nothing but wooden slats to protect them from the fierce wind.

Clutching her rucksack, Little Tiger huddled on the floor and pulled her arms around her body to stop the cold wind gusting through her clothes. Why had nobody told them the climate was so harsh or the land so rugged? Mountains seem to grow out of the sides of rivers, and trees taller than any building she had ever seen formed dense forests on either side of the rail tracks. Most of her friends wore only straw hats and thin jackets and pants. Little Tiger was grateful that she had her warm felt hat to pull over her ears.

Soon she heard the roar of a river and stood up to peer out of the railcar. On one side she saw a wide, fast-moving river. On the other, rising at odd angles along the tracks, were rough wooden stakes — grave markers with Chinese names scrawled on them. Workers had died here in the hundreds. Was her father one of them?

With a huge blast of steam, the train rolled to a stop at Hell's Gate, just past the bustling town of Yale where the river narrowed into raging rapids between the towering walls of the canyon. A railway boss explained that their job was to build the track from there to Eagle Pass to connect with the track coming from the east. They would live in tents that they moved with them as they built the track.

They would build trestle bridges across the rivers and canyons — hundreds of feet high, some a thousand feet long. They would cut tunnels through the mountains — thirteen of them before they reached Eagle Pass. Some workers would clear the forest, some build the bridges, some break up rocks into gravel, some lay gravel to grade the track. When they couldn't go around a mountain, they would chip out a tunnel by hand with their chisels, or blast away its side with dynamite.

What an impossible task! thought Little Tiger. The mountains rose thousands of feet into the heavens on both sides of the river. How could they build bridges up to a thousand feet long? Or dig tunnels by hand through the hardest granite in the world? No wonder the place was called Hell's Gate. Maybe it really was the gate to hell.

They were herded off to the construction camp. There the track came to an abrupt end and, with a sharp whistle, the engine pulled to a sudden stop. Its steam hit Little Tiger, Wang Ma, and her group in the face as they clambered down from their flat car, amid the Chinese foreman's shouts of "Hurry up! Move it!"

She peered through the steam to see the construction site. It seemed that the bosses had train cars of their own at the end of the track — an office car, a dining car, and the house-on-wheels that James had told her about. Even from the outside, it seemed fit for an emperor: the windows had red-velvet curtains and there were brass handles on the doors.

But past these, she was amazed by the buzz of activity in the camp. Hundreds of men swarmed like ants. There was a constant thrum of hammers and chisels. Men were chipping rocks into gravel by hand; others wheeled it away in barrows. Horses pulled wagons loaded with timber and boxes of dynamite. Beyond that were the workers' living quarters, which seemed to be in two parts — one had cabins made of logs, the other was a collection of tents that flapped in the wind. White men clutching metal bowls lined up in front of one of the log cabins and emerged with a steaming dinner. Little Tiger was so hungry that she felt faint at the smell of this food and walked toward the lineup.

A white worker quickly pushed her away. "Hey, kid, where in hell do you think you're going?" he demanded.

Little Tiger pointed to her stomach. "No food for long time."

The worker laughed and pointed far beyond to the tents. "Yellow and white don't mix here, kid. Your kind eat and sleep in those tents over there. And don't get too comfortable. You yellow men are working in the tunnels tomorrow."

Little Tiger looked at the muscular men, Chinese and white alike. Could a puny kid like her survive here? Or would she die from exhaustion and hunger on her first day on Gold Mountain?

She and the men were taken to the work site on horse-drawn carts over a narrow road built of logs. It hugged the mountainside and she couldn't help but peer down into the canyon far below. Every time the cart swayed dangerously close to the edge, Little Tiger felt her heart drop into her stomach. The driver of the cart warned them not to move, telling them that only last week the lead horse had lost its footing and tumbled more than three-hundred feet into the river below. The animals and that entire crew had perished.

But this time they made it, and when they arrived she and Wang Ma were assigned to the same gang. They would live in tents, five men in each, and report to a "bookman" who kept track of their hours and their pay. Each crew also had its own cook and tea boy.

Wang Ma whispered to her, "Good. A *Chinese* cook. Finally, some food we recognize." She answered with a grin, "Finally some *food!*"

At dawn on her first day of work, Little Tiger stood in her canvas shoes with her crew outside the cook's tent, waiting for their congee. Cook was a rough fellow with only one arm and a rough sense of humour to match. He was the first to notice the Chinese man riding toward them wearing Englishman's clothes and sitting tall and arrogant in his saddle. Cook, who was the camp gossip, pointed at him and whispered to the kid, "That's Bookman — be sure to stay on his good side. They say he killed a man in a fight and wears the scar to prove it."

Indeed he did have a scar — a long, ugly one.

There were fifty men in Little Tiger's crew and Bookman wrote each man's name in his ledger. Cook explained that he kept track of every man on the crew, how many days they worked, and how much they spent each week.

"What do you mean 'spent'?" asked Little Tiger.

Cook laughed at the naive boy until his belly ached. "You'll never see a full dollar a day, kid. You gotta learn not to trust these foreigners."

Cook listed the money that Little Tiger would have to spend each week on the job. First of all was a deduction to repay the passage from China to Canada — forty dollars in all. The money would be taken off, a little from each paycheque.

"What! Forty dollars? But they promised passage paid!"

"I told you," said Cook. "Never trust the *gwailo*."

Little Tiger was almost dizzy counting up all the money she would have to pay to the Nichol Railway Company — board: nine cents a day; food: twelve cents a day in summer and seventeen cents a day in winter. If she was sick or couldn't work — no pay. And Bookman himself got one cent a day from every member of the crew.

Cook shook his head. "Nobody on the dock in Hong Kong tells you about the winters here. They're fierce. You'll need blankets, boots, hats, gloves, socks, and medicine. A dollar a day doesn't go far here."

When he told her that the Irish workers got a dollar fifty, sometimes two dollars a day plus free room and board, she almost burst into tears. How could the Mountie on the poster betray them this way? With those blue eyes, he'd promised prosperity in Canada.

Bookman rode up beside Little Tiger and looked her up and down with suspicion. She thought she would be frightened by this man with so much power and a violent past, but in fact she wasn't. Up close, she saw that his scar ran from his forehead down to the corner of his mouth, but his eyes were tired, not hardened and bitter as she imagined a killer's would be.

"What's your name?" he demanded.

"Little Tiger."

He looked at her over the top of his ledger.

"You should be called Bottom of the Barrel. You're little, that's for sure, but I don't see any tiger."

He wet the flat end of a lead pencil with his tongue, poised to record her name, then looked at her again with a little compassion. "You'll be useless in the tunnels and on the tracks, probably even a danger to the others. I'd be surprised if you could even lift a chisel, never mind a railway tie!"

Little Tiger stood her ground. "I am fantastic with black powder."

"Are you?" sneered Bookman, disbelief written over his face. "Where are you from?"

"Ping Wei village."

He paused a moment, frowning. "I know the place," he said. "No good ever came out of Ping Wei."

Little Tiger was about to ask a question about his family but she stopped herself. It was as if the name of her village took him to a dark place.

Bookman turned to Cook. "I have enough men for now. Could you use this boy to wash bowls and deliver tea to the jobsite?"

Cook looked surprised — he'd been asking for an assistant for a long time — and gave an enthusiastic "yes." He turned to Little Tiger and said, "If you're my tea boy, you better call me Powder, like everyone else."

Bookman wrote down *Xiao Hu* in his ledger.

"Thank you, Bookman." Little Tiger bowed to him. "It is true I am little but I am brave."

Bookman made no comment and announced to the crew, "Your first pay is Friday."

The men cheered but Powder gave them a *wait-for-it* look. Bookman continued, "That's when you will see your first deductions — rent, food, and money for the passage from China."

Wang Ma stepped out from the group. "There must be a mistake," he said. "We were told one dollar a day, and passage to Canada paid."

Bookman looked at Wang Ma with disdain. "Don't believe everything you're told."

And with that, he spun his horse around and trotted off. The men grumbled but they picked up their hammers and chisels and moved toward the cart that would take them to the tunnels. Little Tiger watched them go with mixed feelings. Would she ever have a chance to show how fantastic she was with black powder or would she be a tea boy for the rest of her life?

Chapter Seven

Little Tiger would never get used to being with men all the time — working, sleeping, eating, washing. The toilets were little more than stinking holes in the ground. To use them, she managed to slip away alone late at night or early in the morning. She washed herself by reaching under her clothes. Oh, how she longed to slip off all of them and scrub her skin with hot soapy water until every inch of soot and grime was gone but that was impossible, living the way she did, terrified of letting anyone know that she was a girl.

"Who's first?" called Powder, the cook, one morning. He pulled out a stool and lifted his butcher knife high in the air.

Word had come down from the white bosses to Bookman that the Chinese workers should cut off their queues. The *gwailo* didn't understand why Chinese men wore pigtails anyway — weren't they for little girls?

Bookman, who had no queue, gave the order, but workers who wanted to return to their homeland someday resisted. They wanted to keep their queues. They'd had them since childhood, and besides, back in China you could be executed if you didn't have one.

Bookman turned to Wang Ma. "You — sit down. A queue is dangerous when you're blasting dynamite."

Reluctantly Wang Ma sat on the stool and closed his eyes tight. Little Tiger cringed as she watched. With his knife, Powder sawed through the queue that had hung down Wang Ma's back since he was a boy, then he grabbed the braid before it fell on the ground and waved it in the air like a trophy. Wang Ma felt the naked back of his neck and bent his head. Almost everyone knew how he felt; they wanted to go back to China someday, too.

"Next!" called Powder, waving his knife and eyeing Little Tiger. He motioned her over. Horrified, she grabbed her pigtail and ran off to the far side of the tents to hide. She had good reason to keep her hair. One day she hoped to become a woman again. Perhaps then she could look as lovely as her mother in the tintype, with her hair wound in coils, held with fancy combs. There was no way she would let anyone chop off her hair; for her, the queue was a hope that under her slouch hat and neck scarf she was still a beautiful girl with long black hair.

She sat behind a tent and caught her breath. She heard voices and realized that Bookman was close by and a seedy-looking Irishman — the Controller for the Nichol Railway Company — was beside him. He was a bigwig, almost as important as Mr. Alfred Nichol himself or

Edgar, the chief engineer. This controller was responsible for all of the money that came in and went out. He looked around at the tents that had been set up for the thousands of newly arrived Chinese workers. Satisfied that they were alone, he lit a cigar and turned to Bookman.

"With all these new workers, there's bound to be some casualties this week."

Bookman nodded his head.

"Just make sure you get all their names down," the Controller ordered.

Bookman seemed offended. "I know my part," he muttered and patted his ledger.

Little Tiger found it an odd conversation. Of course Bookman would have all the names! He had noted everyone on her crew and she'd seen him write down each name. But now there was no time for her to think about what the Controller meant. Here was her chance, while her crew were having their queues cut off, to visit the grave markers along the tracks close to the camp. Ever since she'd spotted them from the train, she wanted to see if the name Li Man appeared on one of them. It was the last thing she wanted to discover, but it was something she had to do.

She walked along the tracks, checking each marker. Many men, Chinese and white, died doing the dangerous work but the Chinese were never given proper burials. Their bodies were usually covered with a thin layer of dirt and left where they fell, marked only by a simple wooden stake with their names scratched on it. She searched the markers but no, her father's name wasn't here.

Already her quest seemed hopeless. If he was still *alive*, how could she find him among the thousands of Chinese workers? And if he was *dead*, how many markers would she have to read, and how could she get back along the track to find them?

Discouraged, Little Tiger ran back to the cook tent and rinsed the rice under Powder's watchful eye. Little black insects were crawling in the bag and she squashed some of them with the flat of her hand, then boiled the rice for the crew. Wang Ma picked up a mouthful with his chopsticks and made a face.

"What the heck is this?" he asked. "Bugs! Look." He shoved his bowl under Little Tiger's nose and then laughed. "Don't tell Bookman. He'll charge you extra for them."

Little Tiger smiled at the bitter joke and dug into her own rice bowl. Still, she longed for anything fresh — fish or vegetables.

"I wish we had fresh food," said Little Tiger.

Powder laughed at her. "If you want something fresh, boy, you could learn to fish. But there's only one problem. The blackflies will devour you before the fish bite your hook."

The crew went back to work and Little Tiger boiled more water for tea. As she threw in handfuls of loose tea leaves, Powder looked over her shoulder.

"Make it strong," he barked. "I'm sick of the men complaining that it's too weak."

She added another handful of tea leaves, stirred them, and then poured the tea into pails that she balanced on a yoke across her shoulders. She walked carefully over the sharp stone path that led from the camp to the new tunnel where her crew was working.

At the tunnel entrance, Little Tiger set down her pails and watched. It was amazing how they made a hole through a mountain. First they blasted an entrance with nitroglycerine — black powder — then they shored up the sides and the roof with timbers. There was always a danger of the roof collapsing inside the tunnel but the men had to go in anyway, and every day they chipped the granite away inch by inch, carving by hand a tunnel wide enough and high enough for a train to get through. Hundreds of men worked solemnly, silently, concentrating on the dangerous task at hand. Some chiselled away at the rock, others pounded the walls with pickaxes, others carted out the debris. It was slow, back-breaking work, but this new tunnel was almost completed.

Suddenly, there was a loud crack. Little Tiger saw the shoring at the entrance shift and start to buckle. She heard a worker deep inside shout, "Cave-in! It's coming down. Run!"

Men streamed out of the tunnel, screaming with fear. Then there was a rumble, louder than thunder. Dust and rocks shot out from behind the workers as they ran for their lives. Alarm bells clanged through the whole construction site. Little Tiger covered her mouth to stifle a scream as she realized the full horror of the cave-in: many of the workers were likely dead inside, killed by falling rock and wooden supports that had held up the roof of the tunnel. Those who escaped now writhed in pain as they collapsed outside the tunnel. Many of them had had their limbs shorn off when the sides collapsed. Staggering around in a daze, she tripped over something strange and gagged as she realized it was the crushed head of a boy only a few years older than herself. There was blood everywhere, and heavy moaning. She heard a shriek behind her and turned to see that it came from a man in her own crew. She ran to wipe his forehead. He reached out to her, gasped for breath, then turned away, and died.

Bookman called for stretchers to carry the wounded away, as James came running up the hill with Edgar. They stared dumbfounded at the disaster.

"Doctors!" James called out. "We need doctors for these men, and quickly."

Bookman laughed bitterly as he handed Little Tiger some cloth to bind a man's wounded shoulder. "That young Mr. Nichol has a lot to learn. Only his kind get doctors."

Little Tiger looked up at him, objecting. "Mr. James, he is not like the others."

"Ha! What do you know?" snarled Bookman. "The *gwailo* are all the same. They all treat us like animals."

He ordered the wounded to be laid out along the track. There were no doctors to be seen.

Edgar pulled James aside. "Forget the doctors, James. Chinamen have to look after their own. Our job is to deal with this cave-in. Christ! This tunnel is blocked forty, maybe fifty feet back. It'll slow us down for days — maybe weeks."

A few stretchers arrived and Little Tiger helped lift her wounded friends onto them. Others were carried off on their fellow workers' shoulders. Little Tiger looked at the dead men left along the tracks.

She turned to Bookman. "Will these men's bones ever go home?"

Bookman became thoughtful. "Not for a long time," he answered. "I write their names and their home village on a piece of paper and seal it in a jar. We bury that jar with the body. Years later we hope the bone cleaner will come and pack up the bones with the jar and ship them back to their families in China."

"That's good," said Little Tiger. "My mother told me that if their bones are not buried in their home village, the souls of the dead wander forever."

"That is true," said Bookman, nodding.

One of the crewmen began to scatter spirit money over the bodies of the dead. Edgar fidgeted impatiently as he waited for the man to finish his ritual. Soon he yelled, "Enough! Get these bodies out of here. There's work to be done," and called over the dynamite boss.

Little Tiger eyed the huge boulders and the collapsed timbers blocking the entrance to the tunnel. At the bottom she spotted a very small opening. *Ah!* she thought. *I could squeeze in there, I know it.* And she knew what was needed to blast out the debris and leave the tunnel intact. She remembered Mr. Zhou's lesson — the exploding walnut. He'd taught her well.

The Chinese dynamite boss had his orders from Edgar and now he walked toward the waiting men.

"Boss wants a man to clear the cave-in. Will pay good money."

Cheung Wei laughed in his face. "Crawl inside that? Naagh. It's a death trap."

Nobody wanted the job.

The dynamite boss was stone-faced. "Boss will pay five dollars to any man who can set a charge behind this rubble and blow it out."

Edgar added from behind him, "That's a helluva lot of money for fifteen minutes' work."

But even that couldn't convince the workers. Most of them, still bleeding, turned back to the camp. But not Little Tiger. Standing beside Bookman, she was listening hard, and thinking.

James came up to Edgar. "Couldn't we set charges bit by bit from the front and gradually clear out the opening that way?"

Edgar had a quick put-down. "No, the overhead is too unstable. We need to set charges *behind* the rubble."

"But," said James, "the only way in that I can see is the size of a dinner plate."

Edgar had to agree. He watched the workers one by one go back to their tents and barked at Bookman, "Where' s my volunteer?"

Bookman shrugged and pointed to the retreating workers.

"Okay," yelled Edgar, "tell them there's an extra five bucks in it."

What a lot of money! thought Little Tiger. It would pay back everything she'd bought from the company store, and more.

"Sir, I do it!" she piped up.

Bookman grabbed her arm and shook it. "Never mind, you."

But Little Tiger was adamant. "I worked in a fireworks factory in Hong Kong. I know about explosives."

Bookman scowled. "This isn't fireworks, it's dynamite."

She shook herself free from his grip. "I want to do it."

"No, Xiao Hu. I'm not sending your bones home to your parents."

Little Tiger stood tall. "I don't have any parents back home. Let me do it."

James recognized this voice — it was his buddy, the kid. He marched over. "Tiger! Are you crazy in the head?"

Desperate to prove herself, Little Tiger said, "No, not crazy, Mr. James. I get the five bucks. And now I get five bucks extra!"

James sighed. "Okay, fine, if you're so fired up to do it." He eyed Edgar. "Just make sure my little buddy here comes back in one piece."

The dynamite boss gave Little Tiger her equipment — matches, a couple of candles, and a big bundle of explosives all tied together, plus the longest fuse from his arsenal. She put on her bravest face.

"Watch. I am fantastic!" she called out and started toward the entrance.

"Wait!" shouted James. He'd spotted a pair of thick gloves and brought them over to her. "You're going to need these."

Touched by his kindness, Little Tiger pulled on the gloves.

"Now don't kick anything loose, and for heaven's sakes, be careful," he said.

"Yes, Mr. James, I be sure to be careful."

She put all her equipment into a sack and slung it over her shoulders. She squeezed herself into the oh-so-narrow hole and wiggled through, feet first. Before she slid into the rubble, she took a last look back and saw James watching her intently, gnawing at his lower lip.

She closed her mind to the danger ahead and imagined that she was a fish slipping over and around the sharp rocks, as she made her way through the cave-in rubble to the tunnel beyond it. Fallen timber beams crisscrossed the space ahead of her and her feet slipped on loose rock. It was pitch-dark now, and she feared that at any moment more of the tunnel could collapse on her. She lit a match to her first candle and held it high, planning her strategy: there was just room enough for her to move about here, her fuse seemed long enough to do the job safely, and there were her explosives all tied together in one bundle.

Remembering Mr. Zhou's advice, she repeated his words out loud, "It's not how *much* powder you use but *where* you place the charges that counts." She surveyed the fallen tunnel walls around her, the rubble behind her, and made a decision. She would unwind the string that bound all the dynamite sticks together and place them *separately* in five different locations among the fallen rocks at the bottom and the sides of the tunnel. Then she would connect each of their fuses to the main fuse, the long one, and pull it back with her to the entrance where she would light it.

Her first candle was burning dangerously low, so she dripped some wax from it onto a fallen timber just above her to make a glue, then pulled out a second candle, pressed it into the still-hot wax, and lit it. It did the trick.

Now she could see to do her job. She chiselled at a crevice halfway up the rock wall until it was wide enough to wedge in a single stick of dynamite with its fuse dangling from the end. She then inserted the four other dynamite sticks in four separate holes on either side of the tunnel walls, and attached their fuses to the main one.

But cutting through the silence, she heard a strange sound — drip, drip, drip. She looked up and saw small drops of water collecting and falling from the ceiling above. This could be disaster! When the main fuse was lit and the flame rushed along its length, this water could fall onto it and make it fizzle out before it ignited the dynamite sticks she had set so carefully. What could she do?

She gave herself a good talking to. "You are first class," she said aloud. "Nothing can stop you now." But just in case, she prayed to her ancestors to stop the drip, drip, drip from the ceiling.

Carefully, she checked everything, then scrambled back out through the rubble and back out the narrow opening at the entrance.

As she emerged from the hole, the Controller was puffing madly on a cigar while James and Edgar were pacing the railway ties. She wiggled out, unfurling the long fuse from the mouth of the tunnel.

Her big moment! She turned to the men with a grin and took out her matches, ready to light the fuse, but to her surprise Edgar grabbed the cigar from the Controller's mouth and came forward. Usually the bosses were the first to get as far away as possible from the blasts. Not this time.

"Good job, kid," he said. "Now get away. I'm gonna light this one." He pulled on the cigar to get it burning red, then put the tip to the fuse.

"Fire in the hole!" he shouted.

With a fearsome hiss, the flame travelled along the fuse, through the entrance hole until, with a trail of smoke, it disappeared inside. FIVE-FOUR-THREE-TWO-ONE! Utter silence, then a thunderous detonation. Rocks began to spew from the tunnel like cannon shot, Just in time, James pushed Little Tiger to safety behind a granite boulder as the rocks tumbled past, missing the two of them by inches.

Smoke and dust rolled through the air for a long time while they cowered there. Finally there was another silence, a strange silence. Little Tiger looked up at James, then gingerly they stepped out to survey the tunnel entrance.

Bit by bit a beam of sunlight appeared from the far end of the tunnel.

"It's open!" Little Tiger shouted. "I told you I explode fantastic."

Edgar gave her a pat on the shoulder. "I admire your guts, kid." And he handed her the money — five plus five dollars.

Everyone erupted into cheers. Little Tiger shyly smiled up at James. He was looking at her in a new way, respect and admiration in his eyes. She wondered what he saw in hers.

Chapter Eight

With the tunnel open, Bookman slipped away. Little Tiger thought he was a curious creature. Hard as a railway spike, with a fierce temper that could flare at the least provocation, but protective of the men in his crew. She never saw him joke or laugh with either his white bosses or the other Chinese.

Edgar and the Controller, arms around each other, headed toward their office railcar at the end of the track, but James stayed behind.

He nudged her in the ribs. "I bet those two will open the champagne back there. It was a big deal what you did today, little buddy. Saved their sorry butts, you did."

Little Tiger was thrilled by his praise but turned toward the cook tent. "I have to help Powder with dinner now."

"No way," said James.

"If I don't work, I don't get paid."

"Leave it to me," he said. "I'll clear it with Bookman. Besides, you got five bucks plus five bucks extra, right?"

Little Tiger reached into her pocket and rubbed the notes between her fingers.

James grinned at his buddy. "How about I show you a place where I go to wind down."

Little Tiger hesitated.

"Come on kid. I'm the boss."

They walked along the river's edge until James spotted a barely trodden path that led into the dense forest where the trees were so tall that no sun penetrated the canopy. He parted the brush and motioned his buddy to follow closely behind.

"This is where the Indians come to hunt deer and bear," he said.

"I see the Indians sometimes." said Little Tiger. "They fish with their nets and spears. If they have extra, they come into camp and trade their fish for tea. It's good fish, too."

They stepped onto a thick carpet of fallen boughs and needles, picking their way among the jutting roots until they came upon an opening in the forest and a stunning vista of valleys and mountains spread before them. James stretched his arms wide as if to say that everything they saw was theirs.

"Whoo!" he shouted. "Beautiful!

They stood on rocky shale at the edge of a deep mountain pool. James picked up a pebble and skipped it across the surface. Little Tiger crouched on her heels and splashed at the water.

"Do you always come here?" she asked.

"Every chance I get," said James.

She scooped a handful of water and splashed it onto her dusty face. She tensed when the icy water hit her skin and screamed, "Ooo! It's cold."

"Aw, it's not so bad once you get in."

Get in? Ah, he intended that they both go swimming! She turned to see him. He had taken off his boots and was about to strip off his clothes. She wasn't sure whether to stare at this man or turn away. It was clear he intended to take off all his clothes. She'd seen naked men before — lots of them, since it was hard to avoid when you shared tents. But she'd never seen a naked *white man* before. It wasn't so much that it was a white man. She figured men were men and all the parts were pretty much the same, but the thought of seeing the Controller or Edgar buck naked just made her shiver with embarrassment. However, she felt a totally different kind of shiver looking at James strip off his long johns. Blushing, Little Tiger turned toward the water, averting her eyes.

"How deep is it?" she asked.

"I don't know. Ten, maybe fifteen feet. Come on kid. Last one in's a rotten egg."

With that, Little Tiger did turn, and saw the very naked, very fit Mr. James place one foot after the other and clamber up the rocks to a natural diving platform, high above the water.

"Whoo! Look out below!" he shouted, full of glee.

He wrapped his arms around his knees and cannonballed into the pool below. There was a huge splash and Little Tiger waited for him to emerge. Where had he gone? He surprised her by grabbing the back of her shirt and pulling her from behind into the frigid pool.

She gasped as she hit the water. She flailed and kicked, sputtered and gasped. James was surprised. She was in trouble, so he lifted her under the arms and helped her up onto the rocks.

"Why didn't you tell me you couldn't swim?"

She squeezed water from the bottom of her jacket. "I swim fan-tastic!"

"Nope. You swim like a stone."

James gathered up his clothes and pulled on his long johns. Little Tiger checked that her money was safe and hoped the sun and the breeze would dry out her pants and shirt. There was no way she'd take off her clothes in front of this man.

"Boy, I can't get over what you did in that tunnel!" said James. "My father's jaw is gonna drop when he sees that opening all cleared. You did it, Tiger! In fifteen minutes you saved us three days of work. I tell you what — if we weren't halfway to hell up here, I'd take you down to the dance hall in Yale and treat you to all the dances you want."

He sat down beside her and pulled on his pants. "I had the sweetest little filly down there last summer …"

"You had what?" asked Little Tiger, afraid of what she might hear.

"Filly. You know, a hootchy-kootchy girl. Ooh! She really had me going."

Little Tiger awkwardly squeezed water out of her sleeves and tried to bluff a macho reaction. "Oh, yes — a hootchy-kootchy."

"Yeah, she was pretty frisky," said James with a wink.

Little Tiger twisted her pant leg with a vengeance to get out the water and, while she would be loath to admit it, her jealousy. First the woman in pink and now a *broken shoe.*

James gave her a sideways glance. "Those clothes would dry faster if you took them off and laid them on the rocks. Feel how hot they are."

Little Tiger shook her head, no.

"Aww, I get it," said James. "You're nervous about going bare ass."

"Bare … ass? Oh, no. I never go bare ass in China. In China, things are much different."

"You're telling me," he laughed.

A steam engine whistled in the distance. It wasn't long ago that the noise of the iron horse terrified her. She'd been afraid of a lot of things when she first came to Gold Mountain: The callousness of the white men and the dangerous work. She could fall off the side of a cliff or be blown into the river by a badly placed dynamite charge. She might die of sickness, like so many others. It was only late summer but she was already dreading the winter ahead. She couldn't imagine water freezing in the sky and falling to the ground in a blanket of white, but she knew from the old hands that it would happen soon. She heard that in winter, people got frostbite and their fingers and toes turned black, then shrivelled and fell off like pine cones. The wilderness itself — the sheer cliffs, wet mountain stone, black forests, and howling animals — created fear in her and all the others. They came from a land of a hundred shades of green and they breathed hot, wet air.

Little Tiger worried about all of that, but the real terror was something she never shared with anyone. What she feared most was loneliness. When she heard the whistle of the steam engine, it sounded like a forlorn cry for the people and the places she had left behind. It always made her sad.

James jumped up at the sound of the whistle drawing closer. "That will be my father coming back. Thank the Lord I've got good news for him."

He slapped Little Tiger on the shoulder and gave her a brotherly hug. "All due to you, my friend. Race you back."

James ran ahead of her into the bush. She lagged behind him, wishing that she wasn't weighed down by her heavy, wet clothes. But it was a good thing. Little Tiger was afraid that if he touched her again she would want him to hold her for a very long time.

When she got back to her tent the men were already snoring, deep in sleep. Her heart was beating fast as she relived the events of that day. So many exciting things had happened so close together: setting the dynamite in the tunnel, watching the rocks and rubble shoot out, seeing the light appear at the other end, going to the secret swimming hole with Mr. James, sitting beside him, being wrapped in his brotherly hug.

She reached for her satchel and pulled out the photo of her family — her lovely, young mother holding her as a baby on her lap, her father standing tall and proud. Was there a chance that he was still alive? Wouldn't that be wonderful!

***

Early the next morning Bookman told her there was a change in her schedule. She would be delivering tea to a new dynamite crew much higher up on the mountain.

"Why there?" she asked.

"Big boss in big trouble. Mr. Nichol just back from meeting money men. He had to promise them he would finish the next section of track in sixty days."

"But we can't do that in sixty days," said Little Tiger, calculating how far they had come already. "It's too far. It could take four months, maybe more."

"Not when the bosses change the route. Mr. Edgar has ordered us to blast away the side of the mountains, instead of going around them."

Little Tiger was flabbergasted. "The whole side of a mountain? This one is a wall of stone going straight up from the river. How's he going to do that?"

"By killing lots of us," answered Bookman. "He told Mr. Nichol that if he uses lots more Chinese on the dynamite crews they can blow off the sides of the mountains, then they can lay track twice as fast and meet his deadline."

Little Tiger thought about her crew. "Most of these men are farmers. They've never worked with explosives before. What if they blow off their arms and legs? What then?"

Bookman glared at her. "They'll just use more of us."

She felt a sudden chill.

Powder motioned her to pick up her tea pails. "We built the Great Wall of China," he said. "The bosses figure we can do anything."

Bookman shook his head. "No — that would mean respect, and they have none of that for us. Sure, they pay a bit more for setting explosives, but they don't care if we blow ourselves up. But you, Xiao Hu, you should respect yourself! Stop following the boss's son like a pet dog. The *gwailo* will work you to death and then spit on your grave. Their friendship means nothing. Remember this: only Chinese look after Chinese."

Little Tiger picked up her yoke and tea pails and trudged to the site where the new dynamite crew had set up their work station. They had two large wooden hoists from which the hoist crew lowered the blasters down the side of the cliff on swing chairs. She was aghast when she saw that the seats of these chairs were little more than three pieces of wood bound together with rope. She watched the men being lowered in these flimsy chairs, saw them chip holes into the side of the cliff, place dynamite charges inside the crevices, light their fuses, then call out "Fire in the hole!" and pray that the hoist men would crank them back up onto the ledge before the dynamite exploded.

They were working at a dizzying height — more than two hundred feet above the grey, churning river.

If a chair broke or the hoist men were too slow, or the charges went off too early, they'd be blown apart. But nobody seemed to care. The Chinese wanted the money and the bosses wanted the railway built faster to meet the deadline and satisfy the banker who had loaned them the money for the job.

Little Tiger stood beside Wang Ma as he waited for his turn.

"Look at you!" she said. "How'd you get on the dynamite crew while I'm still lugging tea pails?"

Wang Ma shrugged his shoulders as if it were nothing. One day he was a farmer, the next he was packing explosives.

"I volunteered," he said. "I make an extra dollar a day so I can go home early."

Little Tiger raised her eyebrows. "One more buck every day? Wow!"

She noticed the dynamite in Wang Ma's satchel, reached over, took out a bundle of sticks, and examined their fuses. "It's a hot, dry day," she muttered.

"What's that got to do with anything?"

"I worked in the firecracker factory. I know things. These dynamite sticks have short fuses — too short. They burn too fast on a day like this."

Little Tiger spotted Edgar talking to the dynamite boss. She grabbed the dynamite sticks and was heading over to them when Wang Ma pulled her back.

"Don't complain, Xiao Hu. Please. It's an extra dollar a day for me. Don't ruin it."

She stopped in her tracks and stared at him. She saw

how much it meant to him — an extra dollar a day! She thought a moment, then asked him for his cup of tea.

"What for?" he asked.

"Just pass it to me. I need a reason to talk to Bookman."

Puzzled, he handed it over. Bookman had set up a canopy and was working on his ledger, close to the hoist men. Carrying the cup, Little Tiger came up quietly behind him, not wanting to interrupt his concentration. Over his shoulder she could read the columns in the ledger with the crew's names, the amount they were paid, and what they owed. Suddenly Bookman sensed she was there and slammed the book shut, fiercely angry.

"Don't ever sneak up on me again," he snarled. "Do you hear?"

She tried to stay calm. "Sir, I want to work on the dynamite crew."

He shook his head vigorously. "Be a good tea boy and stay alive."

She handed him the cup of tea. He took a swig, handed it back, and shooed her away. Little Tiger vowed to herself that this would be the last drink she served on Gold Mountain. She would find a way to get on that dynamite crew.

Chapter Nine

When her long work day ended and night closed in it was still hot. Little Tiger decided to sneak away herself to the secret mountain pool. She sat on the rocks under a brilliant starry sky and giggled, remembering how scared she'd been when James pulled her into the water. Yes, it *had* been freezing cold but she had also told a bold-faced lie about being a "fantastic" swimmer. She'd never in her life been in water deeper than her knees.

"Hey, you. What's so funny?"

She jumped at the sound of James's voice. He'd come up behind her without her hearing him and she felt almost embarrassed by being at his secret spot. Shyly she confessed that she'd been wanting to come back ever since he'd brought her here.

"I thought you might feel that way," he said. "We seem to think a lot alike."

He sat down on the rock beside her and gazed up at the sky. "Look at all those stars ... I guess you have the same stars over China. I mean, it's not like Australia or some place where the stars are upside down."

Little Tiger laughed out loud. She laughed more with James than she had with anyone. He made her feel different, lighter, as if a weight had been lifted off her.

"The same, yes," she said and pointed right above them. "See that very, very bright star? She's the weaving girl and he's the cowboy."

"Cowboy, huh? Are there cowboys in China?"

"Not exactly, but we like the Wild West. Anyway, a weaving girl from the *spirit* world takes a swim in the river and a cowboy from *this* world steals her dress. Because he sees her naked, she must become his wife. They fall in love."

James shifted uncomfortably on the rock. Little Tiger kept staring into the sky.

"My mother told that story to me. Many nights she looks at the sky, praying that my father will come back from Gold Mountain."

"What happened to him — your father?"

Little Tiger paused. She had a deep urge to share her secret with this *gwailo*, this man so different from her, but so much like her, too. Could she trust him? She decided she could.

"It was a long time ago. First letters came, then no letters. What happened, we don't know."

James leaned in. "Is that why you came to Gold Mountain, kid? So you could find your father?"

Little Tiger nodded, blinking back the tears. "I never really knew him."

There was silence as she relived her emotions. She had never told anyone about the pain of having her father leave when she was so young. She knew he had to go to Gold Mountain but she wished he had come back. If he had, her mother might not have died, she wouldn't be disguised as a boy, and she wouldn't be on this quest to find him, dead or alive. Would James understand all this? Would he realize why she had to do it?

"I hope you find him," he said.

Little Tiger tried to calm herself. "Me too."

James seemed to struggle with his own emotions. "I kinda know the feeling," he mumbled, "about not really knowing your own father. My dad still sees me as some irresponsible playboy, doesn't consult me on any of his decisions. But I've changed. He forgets that I was the one who went to China and brought back the men he needed."

Little Tiger edged a bit closer to him. "I'm glad you came to China, Mr. James."

He gave her a friendly punch in the arm. "And you, kid. You got a lot of guts coming here to Canada."

Little Tiger punched him back and giggled. "I've got respect for your guts, too."

He turned serious. "When we got off the boat and I heard those insults, I never knew people could have such hatred."

"But *you* don't hate us, Mr. James."

"Of course not. We're really all the same. And my God, the risks you've taken …"

They sat in silence again, listening to the night sounds of the forest and the stream rippling over the rocks.

James became earnest. "Ever since I got back from China, things seem different to me somehow. I didn't use to think too seriously about things, but, I mean, look at what we're doing here — pushing a railway through the wilderness. We're changing the world forever, you and me."

Little Tiger looked over at him with longing. He was so passionate about the railway and the future. She wanted to share her hopes and dreams with him, but first she must tell him the truth about herself.

"Hey, listen, buddy," said James, trying to lighten the tone. "Anytime you want me to shut the hell up, go right ahead and tell me."

"Mr. James," she began, and placed her hand gently on his.

He jerked his hand away. "Whoa! What're you doing, kid?"

Little Tiger hadn't planned when or how to tell him her secret but she knew that this moment, under a perfect sky, in their own magical place, might be her only chance. She leaned in close. "Mr. James. I think about you all the time. I have to tell you something."

James jumped up. "What the hell!"

Little Tiger stood up too. Slowly she took off her hat, unwound the scarf around her forehead, and loosened her long braid until her shining black hair fell in cascades around her face and over her shoulders. Quietly and simply she said, "I am a girl."

James's mouth fell open. His breath was taken away as he looked at the beautiful woman standing before him.

"How stupid could I have been?" he said.

"Mr. James …" She moved toward him but he held both hands up as if to protect himself.

"No, no! Stay where you are. Stay right there. I don't even know who the hell you are!"

Tears pooled in her eyes. "I am Little Tiger. Same as before."

"Is this a con? Some kind of trick?"

"Trick? No! I show you I am a girl so I can tell you my feelings."

James pulled at his hair and walked in circles. "You can't stay here."

"Why not?"

Wild eyed, he looked at her as if she were crazy. "Because, goddamnit, we're building a railway here. There are thousands of men here. It's no place for a girl!"

It was Little Tiger's turn to look astounded. "Living on my own in Hong Kong was no place for a girl, either, but I did that. I had no food, I had to eat garbage, and I did that, too. I became a boy because I had to."

"That's different," said James.

"No, what's different is that you say it is all right for a girl to sell herself for hootchy- kootchy but wrong for me to disguise myself to find honest work?"

James was more perplexed than ever. "You listen to me …" he began.

"No!" she shot back. "You listen to *me.* I watch my mother sit and cry and wait for my father to come back to her. I watch her sick and hungry. I work for a stinking pig to make enough money to support her, work for nothing until she die. I cannot live that life again."

James was adamant. "You can't stay here. And that's that."

"Please don't send me back to where I have nothing and no one," Little Tiger pleaded.

James moved away, angry and overwhelmed. "To hell with it!" he said and ran off into the bush.

Little Tiger wrapped her arms around herself and watched him go, feeling entirely alone in the world. In her heart she'd hoped James would wrap her in his arms and tell her he cared for her. Instead he'd run away. She sat under the stars, sobbing, thinking about what to do next.

Eventually she had to make her way back to her tent and crawl onto the sleeping platform next to Wang Ma. Turning away from him, she covered her face and wept. Wang Ma was having his own restless night. He rolled onto his side and gave her arm a reassuring squeeze.

"I know you miss home," he said. "So do I."

She kept her back to him, desperate not to have to explain anything.

***

The next day, she was in despair as she washed the tin bowls for breakfast and waited for the water to boil for the tea. Powder, the one-armed cook, watched her suspiciously. Did he sense what was wrong?

"You wonder how I became a cook?" he asked.

Little Tiger knew the story. Everyone did. Powder was a blaster, a good one, but one hot day on a cliff, the bosses were using cheap dynamite with short fuses in order to save money. The dynamite blew up too soon and his left arm was sheared off by a sharp piece of flying rock.

"I trusted a white man. He told me the fuses were long enough. Now I cook rice. Safer."

Little Tiger tried to lighten the mood. "Only safer when there are no bugs in the rice. This crew is ready to kill you for that."

Powder flashed a rare smile and wagged his finger at her. "Never trust the *gwailo*."

Little Tiger shrugged. "I want to make a life here after the railway."

"Maybe *you* can. Not me. I want to see China again," he said, wiping his one hand on his apron. "You train as a cook, maybe you can stay on after the railway is built."

"A cook?"

"Yes. Mr. Nichol's personal cook needs a helper who speaks good English. There's a fancy dinner planned for some bigwigs."

"He wants me to work in Mr. Nichol's private railcar?"

"Just this once. Maybe you can get a job after that as a cook — and not by accident like me." Powder pointed to his arm and laughed.

Little Tiger was encouraged. Maybe James would change his mind, maybe he wouldn't send her away. She would prove herself, but meanwhile she had to do her tea job. With a lighter step, she headed up the mountain to the blasting site.

Wang Ma sat in his swing chair and shouted at the hoist men to lower him down the sheer cliff. Little Tiger peered over the ledge and watched him, fascinated, as he held tight to the ropes from the hoist that supported his chair. He braced his feet against the cliff and then pushed off, rappelling farther and farther down until he found a crevice where he could place his charges. It looked terrifying — the hoist crew called it "hanging halfway between heaven and hell" — but Little Tiger was eager to give it a try. She trusted her instincts. She knew that she really was fantastic with black powder.

She picked up a bundle of dynamite sticks and examined them. They still had short fuses and again it was a hot, dry day, just like the one when Powder blew off his arm. This time Little Tiger was determined to make her point. She grabbed one of the dynamite sticks, marched over to Edgar and the dynamite boss, and shoved it in their faces.

"Excuse me, sir. These fuses are too short."

Edgar bristled at her effrontery.

"I know things," she continued. "These sticks have short fuses. They burn too fast in weather like this."

Edgar turned to the dynamite boss. "Who rigged these?"

"I did," he answered. "They're regulation length. What does a tea boy know?"

Glaring at Little Tiger, he barked at her in Chinese, "Regulation length. Mind your own business and get your ass back to work."

Little Tiger balled her hands into two fists and was about to curse them both, but they turned their backs on her. Instead, she looked up into the blazing sun and cursed it as she wiped the sweat dripping down her back. "Hot as hell in Hell's Gate," she muttered.

She looked down at Wang Ma on the cliff, watched as he chiselled a small opening, placed his charges and lit the fuse. It sparked quickly and he shouted, "Fire in the hole," waving to the hoist men on the ledge to haul him up.

Little Tiger was alarmed at how quickly the fuse was burning. At this rate, it would light the dynamite before Wang Ma could be lifted back to safety.

"Faster!" she screamed to the hoist men.

There was a huge explosion. Rocks flew into the air and Wang Ma clutched the ropes of his chair, swinging like a rag doll in a cloud of dust and smoke. The rope groaned as the hoist men winched him up to the ledge. Blood seeped from a gash in his leg and he screamed, over and over, "Aiiyaa! I can't hear a thing. Have I lost my leg?"

Little Tiger checked him over. There were really only cuts and bruises. "It's not that bad," she said, and proceeded to wash away the blood and remove shards of rock from his cuts. She then tore off her neck scarf and ripped it into bandages.

Bookman, the Controller, and the dynamite boss were going over blueprints when they heard the commotion and raced over.

Glaring at the dynamite boss, Little Tiger said, "I told you those fuses were too short!"

Wang Ma screamed hysterically, "Am I going to be deaf?"

Little Tiger narrowed her eyes as she stared down at her friend. She was deliberately harsh because she knew that was the only way to ease his fears. "You won't die. Calm down!"

As Wang Ma was carried away, Little Tiger leaned in close to him. "You'll be fine. The herbalist will look after you."

"Get back to work," ordered the dynamite boss.

"I told you," she repeated. "Now you see what short fuses do."

She walked among the workers with her tea pails. They were not allowed to sit down for a break but they drank the tea thankfully. When the pails were empty, she grabbed her yoke and headed back to the camp, walking unnoticed past the Controller and Bookman, who were deep in conversation. Usually she was lost in her own thoughts. Besides, they talked about boring things: surveys, maintaining acceptable gradients, the bars in Yale. But this time she stopped — they were talking about *her.*

"Who's this kid the boss's son brought back?" asked the Controller.

"A nobody. A tea boy," replied Bookman.

"He's too smart by half."

The Controller chewed on his cigar and grabbed Bookman by his lapel. "I'm getting tired of waiting for my share of the money. Let's divvy up the cash. Give me my cut."

Little Tiger wondered what they meant. Divvy up? His cut? Was this some kind of scam that he and Bookman were running? Did it have something to do with gambling? But she couldn't linger. The last thing she wanted was to get herself into more trouble. She hurried down to the kitchen tent to help Powder prepare the midday rice.

Then she saw James coming out of the herbalist tent where Wang Ma was recovering. She grabbed a cup of water to offer him as an excuse to talk with him.

He looked around furtively before speaking. Pretending to look at some reports, he said under his breath, "I couldn't sleep all night thinking about you. I can't let you stay here. The best thing for you is to go back to China before anyone else finds out."

Little Tiger handed him the water. As he drank it, she blurted out her plea. "Since my mother die, I lived as a boy ..."

James kept his eyes on the reports. "There's a train leaving in a couple of days. You should be on it."

She moved nearer, beseeching him. "I lived all that time as a boy and no one found out."

"I did," he said.

"Because I wanted you to! It was my mistake, telling you."

James kicked at the dirt with the heel of his boot. "I don't know what to think. All I know is that you're a woman and it's against the law for you to be here."

"You would send me to jail?"

He shook his head. "Of course not. I could never do

that to you, but if someone else finds out … goddamn it, I've got to get you back to China."

"Why?"

"Because I'm responsible for you."

Little Tiger tensed her entire body. "For me? Why for me? Why not for Wang Ma or the others?"

James suddenly seemed unsure of himself and his voice cracked with emotion. "You saved my life, remember? Way back in Hong Kong. And then I brought you here to protect you from Lei Mo. I can't let something happen to you now."

Little Tiger smiled sadly. "That's all?"

"No, damn it," said James clenching his fists. "Hear me out. You were my best buddy when I thought you were a guy. We shared a lot. Jeez, I admired you! Wanted to be like you. But now I don't know what to think. You say you're the same as before, but now I can only think of you as a woman. A lovely, brave woman." He caught his breath.

Little Tiger felt her heart pounding and her cheeks flushed. James wiped away the sweat on his forehead and averted his eyes.

"But it's too dangerous for you to stay. I have to put you on that train."

"Please," she cried. "Don't send me back to where I have nothing and no one."

She could tell that James was wavering. "Please Mr. James. I don't want to go."

James looked deep into her eyes. A long silence, then he said, "I don't want you to go either."

Little Tiger exploded with joy and relief. "You don't? Then I don't go! And you won't tell. That is enough, for now. Thank you, Mr. James. Thank you!" She bowed repeatedly.

"Don't bow to me," said James scratching his head, unsure of exactly what had just happened.

Little Tiger ran off toward the kitchen tent. "Wait!" he called.

She heard him but she didn't turn back. What if he changed his mind? She was jubilant. There was still a chance for her in Canada. Maybe even a chance for her and James. She ran his words over and over in her mind, "a lovely, brave woman."

Chapter Ten

Fall had arrived and there was less light now. The days were still hot, but the temperature dropped in the mountain nights. Little Tiger had a restless night filled with anxious dreams about her future. It was still dark when she woke up. Some days were scorchers, but the temperature dropped every night. That morning was so cold that she found a layer of frost on her sleeping platform and she could see her breath in the air. She huddled by Powder's kitchen fire, cupping her bowl between her hands to warm them.

Something had been bothering her ever since she looked over Bookman's shoulder and read the names in his big ledger.

"Who is Wu Kai on our crew?" she asked Powder.

He looked puzzled for a moment. "Who?"

"Wu Kai," she repeated. "I thought I knew everybody."

Powder slammed the lids on the pots and spun around. "Where'd you hear that name? Wu Kai is dead. Don't talk about dead men."

Little Tiger couldn't let it go. "Dead? But Bookman has his name on the payroll list in his ledger, plus a Bai Juan and a Shen Tao and —"

Powder whipped a handful of charcoal at her. "Sonovabitch! Listen! They're all dead. Now shut the hell up!"

He returned to his work and Little Tiger tossed more tea leaves into the pot. It didn't seem to matter what she said these days, she was always in trouble with someone.

Suddenly Cheung Wei came running into the camp. "Bad accident!" he shouted. "A man down — on the cliff."

Little Tiger threw down her bowl and ran with Chung Wei and Powder to the cliff edge. Within minutes, hundreds of workers were gathered there. A body lay face down and motionless on an outcropping far below, trapped beneath a huge boulder.

"Who is it?" Chung Wei asked. "He's not from our crew."

Powder peered over the ledge. "You're right. That's Di Hong. He was on the crew cutting timber for the rail ties. Shouldn't be here."

Little Tiger clamped her hand over her mouth in shock. That was Di Hong down there? "This was no accident," continued Powder. "He had lots of enemies here — they knew he was one of Lei Mo's gang back home."

She hardly recognized the shrivelled figure below as the bully who blew up her market stall and then fingered her to Lei Mo back in Hong Kong. Life on Gold Mountain had been especially hard on him.

***

It didn't take long for the bosses to show up. Edgar coolly surveyed the scene.

"I guess *he* won't be going to work today. How the hell did that Chinaman get himself down on that outcrop?"

"Probably drunk," speculated the Controller, "wandering around in the dark. Maybe he jumped. Homesick. We've lost some that way."

Edgar paced, anxious for the crew to start their work day. "Come on people. That's enough gawking. Chop chop! Back to work now!"

Silently, the workers looked at each other and no one moved. Wang Ma was the first to lay down his shovel. Then one by one, the others threw down their tools. The wheelbarrow workers stood idle, the hoist men halted on the ledge, no one got onto his swing chair. Even Little Tiger put down her yoke and let the tea pails drop into the mud.

"What the hell's going on?" ranted Edgar.

Bookman came forward. "Bad luck. Body must come up or no one will work."

"Goddamnit, that'll take half the day, maybe more."

Bookman threw up his arms. "That's your problem."

The workers glared at Edgar and no one budged. Affronted, he dispatched the Controller to tell James and his father, while the crew stood silent. In a few minutes the two of them came puffing up the hill to join Edgar and Bookman. They surveyed the scene — the striking workers, the body down below. Mr. Nichol clenched his fists and hissed, "We're not going to be held hostage by a bunch of superstitious Chinamen!"

"Why don't we just hoist the body up and get it over with?" suggested James.

Bookman peered over the ledge. "Not so easy. Body is under a rock."

"No matter how long it takes, we've got to get that body up," said James.

Edgar smirked at this. "Why don't we take the week off, James, and have a fancy funeral service?"

Suddenly Mr. Nichol gasped and clutched his chest, his face distorted. Alarmed, James whispered to him, "Are you all right, Father?"

With trembling hands, Mr. Nichol reached into his pocket, took out a small pill box, and popped a white pill into his mouth.

"Of course I'm all right," he barked. "No one stands between me and building this railway. Tell your damn Chinamen that no food or supplies are coming into this camp until they get back to work. Not one goddamned noodle!"

"What?" said James.

"I don't care what happened here. Just get these little bastards back to work."

"Look, Father," said James, trying to control his voice, "they can't be expected to work with a corpse staring at them. Bookman tells us it's really bad luck to leave a body there."

Mr. Nichol's voice rose and his face reddened. "Tell your precious Chinamen that white men die on the job too!"

James drew himself up, inches from his father's face. "But not one of *them* is rotting on a ledge under a rock. And how many dead Chinese *are* there? A helluva lot more than those white men, but who keeps track of *them*? No one."

"Mr. Edgar! Mr. Edgar!"

"What the …?" Edgar turned to see Little Tiger calling his name.

"I will bring body up. Fast. Fast."

Sneering at the kid, Edgar asked, "And how much do you want this time, boy?"

Little Tiger bowed her head. "No pay. I do it for … for respect of many Chinese who die here."

She looked to James for support. She thought he might be proud of her. Instead, he looked horrified. Why? She was fantastic with black powder and this was a job that needed to be done. For the Chinese workers. For Mr. James's railway. James looked between his father and Little Tiger, as if weighing his wrath against her safety.

"Maybe send someone with more experience," he said.

"I don't see any other volunteers, James," said Edgar, pointing to the workers. He turned to Little Tiger. "I don't give a damn why you need to go down there. Just do it and don't take all day."

James sidled up to her and whispered, "Please be careful. And … thank you."

She nodded at him and turned her attention to the task ahead. The outcropping was a long one and just wide enough for her to stand beside Di Hong's body pinned under the boulder. She couldn't think about James now, she needed to remember everything Mr. Zhou had taught her.

She thought back to the lesson about the walnut. She needed to explode the shell without harming his body — the nut. She prayed that the ancient Mr. Zhou's spirit would guide her.

She shouted at the dynamite boss, "I need twenty sticks of dynamite and an extra rope."

The dynamite boss looked to Edgar, who in turn looked to Mr. Nichol for approval. He gave an exaggerated sigh and said, "For God's sakes, give the kid whatever he needs and get this over with."

James helped Little Tiger tie the end of the extra rope to the hoisting mechanism.

"What do you need this for?" he asked.

"It's my hand rope," she said, "to tie around Di Hong and bring him up." And she slung her knapsack, filled with dynamite and matches, onto her back.

"Promise me you'll get out of there quick, as soon as you set the charges," said James, giving her shoulder a squeeze.

"Don't worry. I know what I'm doing, Mr. James."

Grim-faced, she sat on her swing chair. The hoist crew lowered her to the body as James reeled out the hand rope. On the way down, she thought about Di Hong.

He'd been a snitch and a thug, her enemy. But what mattered now was that in death he be treated with respect.

She reached the outcropping where his body lay and looked down into the river, feeling slightly woozy and sick to her stomach. *You must do this*, she told herself. *Remember Mr. Zhou. Remember the lesson of the walnut.* Slowly, she eased herself off her swing chair and felt for a solid foothold on the outcropping.

She heard Wang Ma scream to her, "Stay in your chair!"

"Do what he says!" shouted James.

Little Tiger ignored their warnings. She needed to get to the body. She inched along the ledge, pressed tightly to the mountain side. Pebbles from above rained down on her head. Her breathing was ragged. She saw that the boulder was trapping Di Hong's body from his waist down to his ankles. She bowed to him first, then, making a noose of the hand rope, tied it securely around the upper part of his body — under his arms and around his chest.

She went over her plan. Clearly it was impossible to explode the huge boulder without the two of them being blown to smithereens. What she'd have to do — and this would be really tricky — was to blast away the ledge from *under* Di Hong and leave his body untouched. But would the rope around his body hold? Could she jump back into her swing chair and get up top in time?

She went about setting her many charges on the ledge, checked the rope around Di Hong, then took a deep breath. This was it! She lit the fuses and leaped onto her sling chair, hollering "Pull! Pull me up!"

She heard James repeat, "Bring him up! Move, damnit!"

Bookman's voice rang through the canyon. "Fire in the hole!"

Inching up the cliff, Little Tiger looked over her shoulder at the body, counting down the seconds as the fuses sizzled.

"FOUR, THREE, TWO …" Her feet touched the ledge up top. There was a thunderous explosion below, and she felt herself toppling backward from the force of the blast. Someone grabbed her hands and pulled her forward onto the ledge. It was James.

Debris shot into the air. Smoke and dust obscured everything. Trembling, she clung to James.

"This time, you save *my* life," she said.

As the smoke cleared, they pulled away from each other. Workers rose from their cover and everyone hurried to look over the edge. Below them, the outcropping was gone and Di Hong's body swung eerily in the air from Little Tiger's extra rope. The hoist crew hauled him up and untied the rope. They covered Di Hong's face with a cloth and the stretcher bearers carried him away.

Only then did the workers, one by one, nod respectfully to Little Tiger and pick up their tools. Bookman patted her on the back as Mr. Nichol and Edgar shook hands and congratulated each other on handling the crisis.

James turned to Little Tiger. "That was pretty amazing."

"Do you remember, Mr. James? Di Hong worked for Lei Mo."

Clearly James was puzzled and taken aback. "You risked your life to save a criminal like him?"

"His soul would be trapped, like his body. I did it for him, for my friends, and for the railway. I know you have to finish by your deadline."

"You're something else, that's for sure. I learn something ..." James smiled, "*fantastic* about you every day."

Offering a slight smile in return, she whispered, "Can I stay now for sure?"

She could tell that James was holding back in front of his father and the others. She sensed he wanted to hold her in his arms, but instead he gave her a roughhouse hug, then turned to walk back to the office with his father.

Tossing his cigar butt away, the Controller said to Bookman, loud enough for Little Tiger to hear, "This kid is trouble. Keep an eye on him."

It was almost sunset when Little Tiger went to see the marker just put up for her old foe, Di Hong. She was surprised to see James standing there. They were alone — a rare event.

James said, "The Controller seemed to think this wasn't an accident."

Little Tiger didn't want to answer. There were lots of strange things in this strange land.

"Maybe he missed home too much," she said.

"And jumped?" said James, incredulous.

"It is hard here, Mr. James."

They wandered among the grave markers.

"Many times I think, is my father buried somewhere here, or ..."

James saw the hope in her eyes. "You think he might be alive?"

Little Tiger did still hope, but nobody seemed to have heard of him. "Maybe he work in a mill or on another crew."

James didn't look optimistic.

"Or maybe I find his marker," said Little Tiger. "Send his bones back to China. We have a saying, 'fallen leaves return to their roots.' His bones must go home."

"How could you do that?" asked James, eyeing the new markers.

Little Tiger pointed to them. "With body, they bury a jar with paper inside. On paper Bookman writes name of person and name of village. Six years, maybe more, bone collector comes to unbury what is left of body, clean bones, and send them back to person's village. Chinese people believe soul stays with the body. If the body stays here, soul is lost, will wander forever."

"Do you remember him? Your father?"

"No, not much," she answered. "But I have picture. I can show you."

James smiled at her with a tenderness she hadn't seen before. "I'd like that," he said. "Why don't you bring it to my railcar tonight?"

He reached for her hand and she slipped it into his.

***

Outside her tent, Powder pulled her aside. "That was good what you did today … you deserve something. It's payday. Come join us in the gambling tent. Some fan-tan, maybe some mah-jong? I will give you a stake."

Little Tiger thanked him. She didn't gamble, besides she had better plans."Powder, instead, can you make me a hot bath?"

Powder was not only an inventive cook, but he'd made a bathtub from one of the Irish crew's empty whiskey kegs. Little Tiger had never used it, fearing that one of the men might catch her out, but this time they were all busy setting up the gambling tents. Happily, Powder poured hot water and a herbal essence he'd made himself into the tub. The *gwailo* had laughed at the Chinese men in their tubs with the "girly" scents, but it was a long tradition that the men valued. After her treat — the luxurious bath all alone — Little Tiger put her photo into her jacket pocket and sneaked away to James's railcar.

It was dark now and she knocked quietly on his door. James opened it and looked around to make sure that no one saw them, then ushered her inside. He whispered, "I wasn't sure you'd come, but I sure am glad you did."

He devoured her with his eyes. "How did I ever, ever, think you were a boy?"

Little Tiger laughed but wriggled away and went over to the kerosene lamp. "I have picture to show you." She pulled the tintype out of her jacket and pointed to the worn image. "This is my father, here."

James studied the face of the Chinese man, his wife, and the child.

"This baby? Is that you?"

She nodded and handed the photo to him to study, as she looked around the opulent surroundings. The rail-car had all the fixtures of a grand room: lead-fronted cabinets, velvet upholstery, panelled walls.

"Your mother was a real beauty. You take after her," said James.

Little Tiger frowned and shook her head.

He was confused. "What?"

"I do not feel beautiful, dressed this way."

James put down the photo and moved close. "But without this …" he said, plucking off her slouch hat.

Little Tiger was startled by a noise outside. She walked to the window and drew back the curtain. "Your father. Is he here?"

James turned her around and drew her close to him. "No. He's gone off to Victoria to talk to the banker, Mr. Grant, about getting another loan. But that's business and being here with you is pure pleasure."

He cupped her chin in his hand and stared so deeply into her eyes that she felt they would melt into each other. He lifted her face and leaned in to kiss her.

Little Tiger lowered her head and hesitated. "Mr. James …"

"Just James," he said.

"James," she murmured.

His lips touched hers, tentatively at first, and then with more passion. She had strange new feelings. She couldn't believe she could want him this way or surrender herself to him so completely. All she could think about was her longing to touch and be touched. She lifted her arms around his neck and gave herself completely to his kiss.

Silently, James unwound the scarf around her head. He took her hand and led her toward his bed, unfastened the closures of her jacket and gently pulled it off, then reached for a pillow and placed it underneath her head. They lay together, legs entwined, hands exploring each other. She was not afraid. It was as if she was meant to be here with him. He ran his lips down her neck, lingering in the hollow beneath her chin. His hands ran over her shirt and under it, caressing her breasts as she arched her back, losing herself to the touch of his gentle hands. He reached down and pulled at the strings of her waistband but she caught his wrist and whispered, "No, please ..."

James brought his hand to her face and moved aside a wisp of her hair that had fallen into her eyes. "Whatever you wish," he said. "Mmm. You smell wonderful. Like meadow flowers."

She gave him small kisses up and down the length of his neck and they touched in ways that Little Tiger had never imagined. His kisses lingered on her lips and his touch burned through her clothing. It was all so new, so strange, and the wonder of it swept over her.

"I want you so badly," said James, snuggling into the curve between her head and her shoulders. "I care for you more than any woman I've ever known."

She twisted a lock of his hair. "You are a good man, Mr. James."

He looked at her sternly. "It's just James, remember?"

"James," she corrected herself with mock seriousness. She looked around the railcar and broke into a smile. Here she was — her real self, in this luxurious room, in the arms of a man who cared so much for her. She swept her arms wide with joy. "All this is like dream. Imagine if one day you and me, we have our own railcar."

She snuggled closer into him, giggling, but James became thoughtful. He traced his fingers along her collarbone. "We'll go back to China together and build railways. Live like royalty."

Li Jun sighed. "I could be your queen."

"That would be something," said James, giving her a long, sweet kiss.

They lay together until the moon was high in the sky. James had fallen asleep but Little Tiger dressed and picked up the photo of her family. She looked from the faces of her parents to the *gwailo* sleeping soundly in his bed of fine linens. What would they think of him? What would they think of *her?* She pulled a blanket up over James's shoulders and slipped away, savouring the happiness she had felt in his arms.

Quietly, she crept out of the shadows of the railcar and hurried across the open fields to her camp. The lanterns were lit inside Powder's gambling tent and men were still gathered around the fan-tan table as she entered. Powder lifted up an overturned rice bowl. Dried beans spilled across the table top. Using a chopstick, he sorted the beans into fours as the gamblers looked on.

Wang Ma turned to Little Tiger. "Where've you been?"

"Out for a walk," she replied.

Looking behind her, out to the camp, she caught sight of Bookman stopping by a worker's fire. Cheung Wai followed her gaze and laughed. "Wonder if Bookman ever gets any joy out of life. Maybe he has a shrew of a wife like mine who makes him send home every penny!"

Powder, concentrating on the game, said, "Bookman has no one."

"How'd he get that scar — really?" asked Wang Ma.

"From a fight. He killed the guy."

"Killed a white guy?" exclaimed Cheung Wai.

Powder slapped him over the head. "Don't be crazy! If he killed a *white* guy, the cops would be after him. No, he killed another Chinese. The guy was jumping his claim in the gold-mining camp and Bookman slit his throat. Back home, he's a wanted man. He has to stay here."

Little Tiger froze. Could the man who Bookman killed be her father? Was *that* why no one knew about Li Man?

Powder slammed the upside-down rice bowl on the table. "Stop talking and place your bets!"

Little Tiger wasn't interested and it was very late. She could hardly wait to get to bed in her empty tent. There was so much she had to think about.

Chapter Eleven

It was another restless night for Little Tiger. She was still trying to sleep when the men stumbled into the tent, some celebrating their winning in the game, some irritated because they'd lost. Wang Ma was the worst of the bunch. His sadness ran deeper than the others and he kept nudging Little Tiger as she tried to sleep.

"We will go home together, yes?"

"Go to sleep, Wang Ma. You'll need your wits about you tomorrow."

The next morning, Powder greeted her with the news that she would be helping Mr. Nichol's cook that afternoon. His eyes lingered on Little Tiger's soiled jacket and grimy neck scarf.

"Ask him for some of the serving boy's clothes. The tea is ready. Take it."

Little Tiger weaved in and out of the workers grading the track, stopping to pour tea into their tin cups.

She spotted James and Edgar on their horses. Here was her chance to ask James her new questions about Bookman. She called out, "Mr. James!"

Edgar was taken aback when James broke into a broad grin and rode over to the boy. Little Tiger looked up at James, and said, "I need to talk to you."

"Yeah, sure. Are you all right?"

But at that moment the whistle of the train coming back from Victoria interrupted them as it ground to a stop nearby. Bookman rode up and shouted, "Put down your tea pails, Xiao Hu, and go help with the unloading. "

Little Tiger stood still, looking at him.

"What are you staring at, boy?"

Little Tiger was focusing on his scar. It had new meaning for her now. Could it be that this man was her father's killer? She laid down her yoke, gave Bookman a look of pure hatred, and started toward the loading dock.

Behind the engine, the passenger railcar squealed to a stop in a cloud of steam. James and Edgar dismounted from their horses and stood at attention as Alfred Nichol swung down the steps from the railcar. She watched them greet him.

"Welcome back, sir," said Edgar, extending his hand.

Nichol surveyed the rails ahead. "Are you laying track?"

James took the lead. "Yes. We're back on schedule, Father."

Nichol seemed pleased with himself. "Mr. Grant has

agreed to fund us more money for the project and he's come out to see our progress for himself."

George Grant, a pompous-looking man with a broad chest and a thick head of hair, came down the steps of the passenger car and pumped James's hand.

"Mr. Grant. What a pleasant surprise!" said James. "I haven't seen you and your charming wife since my parents' party, just before I left for China."

Mr. Grant winked at him. "As I recall, you spent a great deal of time with my daughter Melanie at that party. But I'm not the surprise, young man. Look up there."

Little Tiger looked at the same time as James did. There, bursting through the passenger car door, was a blonde-haired woman, wearing a pink fitted jacket and long ruffled skirt. James looked shocked. "Melanie!"

She broke into a giggle at his amazement.

She lifted her skirts and took James's hand as she reached the bottom step, then stood on her tiptoes and planted a lingering kiss on his cheek.

Little Tiger dropped the bag of rice she was lugging. Where had she seen that woman before? Ah, yes! She was the pink fluff woman who had greeted James so warmly at the immigration shed when they first arrived from China. She was dressed in pink again, but what was she doing here?

"Fancy seeing me here, James Nichol," cooed Melanie. "I bet I'm the biggest surprise you've had this week."

James gulped hard and Little Tiger hoped it was because he was thinking about her in his arms the night before. Or was he so entranced by this vision in pink from his *real* life that he had already forgotten about her?

Hurt and confused, she moved in closer. Alfred Nichol was directing his banker to the office railcar, as he turned to James. "While we discuss the financials, I'm sure you'd like to show Melanie around the site."

James looked over to Little Tiger, who promptly and loudly kicked a bucket into his path. Sidestepping it, James adjusted his collar and cleared his throat. "Um, the site? Father, I don't think Melanie would be interested in —"

Melanie smiled brightly. "Oh? Who says I wouldn't welcome the opportunity to spend some private time in the wilderness with James Nichol."

Mr. Grant chuckled and James's father had the parting words. "Look after her well, son."

Melanie leaned into James and linked her arm with his. She held her pink parasol aloft and, in her dainty, laced-up boots, picked her way carefully along the track. Little Tiger followed behind, pushing a wheelbarrow laden with supplies, struggling to get close enough to hear what they were saying.

"The line follows this elevation for another quarter mile before it starts to climb through the narrow canyon," droned James as if he were giving a lecture.

Little Tiger nearly gagged as Melanie feigned interest in his explanation. "Really? Do tell."

"The crew will grade the land with gravel and dirt, then lay the steel rails. After that the fellows from the spiking crew will set the pins."

Melanie gushed, "My! You're turning into a real

railway man."

His voice turned cold. "That's what we're doing out here. I thought you were interested."

"I am!" she insisted, lifting her face to him. "I like seeing you so passionate. It's very attractive." She ran her fingers along his arm and giggled. "I'm not used to seeing you work up such a sweat over steel rails and a lot of gravel."

"It's important work, Mel," said James. He stiffened and walked a little more quickly, leaving Melanie to catch up.

"Absolutely," she said.

Little Tiger could follow them no farther or it would look suspicious. She nearly tipped the wheelbarrow as she manoeuvred it away, all the while watching James lead Melanie to the middle of the trestle bridge that spanned the width of the canyon. It was one of the most glorious views on the work site — snow-peaked mountains in the distance, acres of virgin forest, and the massive river below. She hoped Melanie would catch her heel on a spike and plunge into the abyss.

***

At the kitchen tent, Little Tiger lifted a bag of rice from the wheelbarrow and thumped it onto the ground. Powder was furious. "Hey! You're gonna split those bags wide open. Hurry, Mr. Nichol's cook expects you."

Little Tiger wiped her sleeve across her face, trying to stop the tears brimming in her eyes. Was there something deeper between this woman and James? What else didn't she know about this man she cared for so much? Maybe Bookman was right — never trust the *gwailo*. What would she find out by helping with the dinner party?

In the kitchen of Alfred Nichol's private railcar, Little Tiger scrubbed and peeled vegetables. When his cook wasn't watching, she stuck some raw carrots into her pockets. She'd save them to eat, maybe even trade them for money. The crew was always complaining that there weren't enough fresh vegetables to eat and their teeth were falling out. The kitchen was wedged between the dining car and the office car where the men — Mr. Nichol, Mr. Grant, Edgar, and the Controller — were poring over blueprints and papers. Head down, appearing to be absorbed in her work, Little Tiger could overhear everything they said. Edgar proudly described their progress.

"We still have to blast this section here, but it's primarily soft shale. With the pace we've set, we'll hit our mark bang on deadline."

"That's all very good," said Mr. Grant, "but I'm a money man, and I need to see the financial reports and the ledgers from all the bookmen."

The Controller drew hard on his cigar and paced back and forth nervously. He signalled to Edgar who rolled up the maps.

"Certainly we can look at the financial aspects, if that's what you'd like, Mr. Grant. But you put in long hours at the bank and you've been cooped up all day on that train. We only have so much daylight left, and a ride down into the canyon at sunset will put the soul back into a man. The books will be here tomorrow."

"And so they will," said Mr. Grant, nodding to Mr. Nichol, and together they left to get horses saddled up for the scenic ride.

Mr. Nichol's cook yelled at her and Little Tiger jumped to attention.

"Keep your mind on your work, boy. We need more wood for the oven. Quick! Go get it."

Little Tiger took a canvas sling to fetch the wood and pondered what she had heard. Why would the Controller be so nervous about showing the reports and ledgers to the banker? The bookmen for each crew kept track of the pay and the charges for their men. All the Controller had to do was match up money coming in and money going out. She shrugged. One more mystery of the *gwailo.*

She'd better hurry or this cook would be complaining just like Powder did. She scurried to the woodpile at the side of the train and started filling her canvas sling.

James was standing there pacing, already dressed for dinner in a black evening jacket. Little Tiger had never seen him smoke before but he was puffing furiously. He looked around to make sure no one was watching, then tried to embrace her, but she held him away with both her arms.

"What's the matter?" he asked, clearly taken aback. "Last night you wanted me to keep holding you and this morning you asked to talk to me. "

"Go away. I have work to do," she said.

"But you wanted to talk to me."

Little Tiger sighed. "I am all right. I look after myself. I always have. I can still." She picked up the sling filled with wood and moved around him.

"Wait!" he pleaded.

Little Tiger threw down the bag of wood. All her anger spilled out. "That woman. Is she your wife?"

James threw his hands up in the air. "So that's what this is about. My *wife*?"

"You never think to mention her."

"I don't have a wife!"

"Is she your almost-wife?"

James stubbed his cigarette into the ground. "Melanie … she doesn't matter."

"Doesn't matter?" shouted Little Tiger. "Like the hootchy-kootchy in Yale?"

"Hold on! You stop that right now. You're not allowed to use anything against me that I told you before I knew you were a woman."

"Why? Do you say one thing to men and another thing to women? Either way, hootchy-kootchy girls don't matter, Melanie doesn't matter. So, do *I* matter? "

James was furious. "Of course you matter. I don't want to fight with you over some stupid girl."

"Don't call her stupid!" screamed Little Tiger.

"Jesus Murphy! How could I ever have thought you were a guy? You women all see things screwy."

Little Tiger kneeled down to gather up the fallen wood. "I must go now."

James picked up a log and placed it in her bag,

offering to carry the load.

"We can't talk now," she said.

"Then meet me at the pool at eight o'clock."

She looked at James sadly. "No," she said, and rushed off to the kitchen.

She changed into the uniform that the cook gave her, smoothing her hands along the crisp white jacket.

Melanie arrived in a stunning gown, with her father in a formal evening jacket. She handed her wrap to Little Tiger without a glance or a thank you, and stood waiting for the admiration of the men assembled in the railcar. She was, Little Tiger had to admit, attractive ... for a white woman. Her skin was fair and she showed off her curves in a brocade dress with a plunging neckline.

"Welcome, welcome!" said Mr. Nichol, greeting them warmly. "By Godfrey, you are a beautiful girl, Melanie."

He graciously kissed her hand and she looked to James, who politely pulled out a chair for her at the dining table. They were all seated when Little Tiger entered the room with a soup tureen. James nearly fell off his seat as she ladled the salmon chowder into their bowls. The conversation between Nichol and Grant was jovial, but Melanie was silent and James answered questions from his father in grunts. It was a seven-course dinner and there were polite murmurings around the table about the excellent food and fine wines being available here in the middle of nowhere. Little Tiger cleared the plates, relieved that she hadn't spilled soup on Miss Melanie or dropped a venison chop on James's lap. She'd thought of doing both.

Mr. Nichol turned to Melanie and asked, "What did

you discover on your walk with my son this afternoon?"

James shifted in his chair. Melanie held her head high and, keeping her gaze on James, answered: "I came thinking this would be a romp. I only came for a laugh. But it appears that the laugh was on me."

James reached across the table to take Melanie's hand. "It's just that I wasn't expecting you," he said quietly.

"Apparently not," she said. "It seems, Mr. Nichol, that your son has fallen in love with Chinamen. Now, if you will excuse me, I know you gentlemen want to discuss finance, so I'm going to find my way back to my railcar."

All of the men folded their napkins and stood up.

"I'll see you out," offered James.

"Please don't be silly," she said. "What's the worst that could happen to me alone in the wilderness? I get snatched up by bears or wolves or love-starved Chinamen?"

Livid with anger, she flounced out of the car. Mr. Grant sat back down in his chair, stunned. James jumped up and followed her. Little Tiger dumped the dishes in the wash basin and opened the window so that she could listen to the conversation out there, though she really didn't need to, they were shouting so loud that she could hear them easily. Melanie rushed down the stairs of the railcar, lifting layers of ruched silk and chiffon. From the door, James called out, "Will you please just come back inside!"

As she was stomping off across the uneven ground, the heel of Melanie's shoe suddenly snapped off. "Damn it all to hell!" she cried, yanking off the shoe and throwing it at James.

Little Tiger watched it fly by, almost hitting him in the head.

He picked it up. "Melanie, please don't be like this," he begged.

"Like what? What did I do to be treated so shabbily?"

James hung his head and walked toward her. "You didn't do anything. It's me. I've changed. We just want different things, that's all."

By now Mr. Nichol and Mr. Grant had come out and were standing on the gallery while Little Tiger was almost hanging out the window, watching and listening.

Melanie looked at James, both angry and puzzled. "Different, how? I thought we had ..."

Now it was James's turn to be confused. "Had what?"

Mr. Grant rushed down the steps, interrupting. "An understanding, young man."

Melanie put her hand on her father's arm to restrain him. "Please, Father. Don't. That would be far too humiliating. Clearly, all we have is a *mis*understanding."

She snatched her shoe from James and slipped it on, without the heel. Summoning up as much dignity as possible in the situation, she turned to his father. "Thank you, Mr. Nichol, for just a lovely evening. Good night."

Little Tiger watched as she hobbled off to her own railcar.

Mr. Grant was red in the face as he confronted James. "Young man, I could sue you for breach of promise!"

Melanie screeched from a distance. "Father! Don't

you dare."

James raised himself to his full height and stared at Mr. Grant. Gently but firmly he said, "With all due respect, sir, I didn't promise your daughter anything."

Mr. Grant smiled snidely. "Well, I didn't promise your father anything, either." And he walked away to join his daughter.

By this time even the cook was listening to the drama unfolding outside, and he wasn't one to keep his opinions to himself. "This is a bad thing. Now Mr. Grant won't give the extra money to finish the track because Mr. James doesn't want to marry Miss Melanie," he said. "Back in China, we marry who our parents say. Do you have a wife waiting at home, Xiao Hu?"

Little Tiger shook her head. "No, no wife," she told him. *No husband either*, she told herself.

The cook was right. They listened as father and son raised their voices to each other.

"We don't need Grant's extra money," insisted James. "And we're not going to beg for it. We have a signed loan agreement with the bank and so far we're not in breach of our contract."

"Don't be a fool, James," said his father. "We will be, by the end of the week. We'll never get that track finished in time. One inch short and they'll take everything we own."

James was adamant. "No, they won't. Because we won't let them."

"You don't know that and neither do I," shouted Mr. Nichol and he charged up the stairs with James following. No sooner was he through the door than his knees buckled and he collapsed in a heap on the floor. He fumbled in his vest pocket.

The cook turned to Little Tiger. "It's his bad heart again."

"Aw, shit!" cried Alfred Nichol. "Where are my damn pills?"

James kneeled beside him and dug the pill case out from his vest pocket. But it was empty. He called out for water and Little Tiger came running with a glass. She could see the panic in his face.

He offered the water to his father. "You need a doctor," he said firmly "I'm taking you to Yale."

He whispered to Little Tiger, "I'll be back as soon as I can."

She saw how serious this was. "I hope your father will be all right," she said.

After clearing up in the kitchen, Little Tiger said good night to the cook and hurried back to her tent. Her thoughts were all about James and Melanie … and her. She was heartsick. If James didn't want to marry Melanie, then who did he want to be with?

Chapter Twelve

Next morning she stood in the kitchen tent as Powder examined the supplies that had come in from Yale. He shook his head in dismay at the paltry offerings of rice, dried fish, and staples. He lifted the lid off of a bucket of lard and screwed up his face in disgust. "This is rancid! How the hell can I feed men with food not fit for pigs! Little Tiger, get Bookman over here, now!"

Little Tiger smelled the lard and felt her stomach turn over. She sometimes dreamed of fresh greens and meat in her noodle bowl but, after months of working at Hell's Gate, she knew that the Chinese had no time for dreams; they were too busy surviving.

She wanted to ask Bookman some questions, but first she had to find him amid the constant din of saws cutting trees into ties, of hammers driving spikes into rails, of men yelling out instructions. One of the workers pointed to a supply cart waiting to be unloaded. Over the top of it, she caught a glimpse of Bookman's distinctive black hat. His head was bobbing up and down as he gestured wildly. Who was he talking to with so much animation? Usually Bookman was a man of few words so it was always hard to tell what he was really thinking.

She stood on the far side of the cart, hidden from them, waiting for a break in their conversation. Now she recognized the other voice. It was the Controller. She'd taken a dislike to him the first time she saw him. He had a hard-edged Irish accent and spoke dismissively to everyone but his own bosses. And he looked mean — his mouth pinched tight and his eyes close together like a rat's. His hair and beard were scraggly and his clothes unkempt. She often smelled alcohol on him, which reminded her of Mr. Relic, except that she was fond of that old scoundrel Relic. He'd been like a substitute father in Hong Kong. It still made her sad to think that the reason James brought her to Canada was his murder. She wondered what Mr. Relic would think about everything that had happened to her since.

She stopped daydreaming when she heard the Controller's voice rise.

"I told you this would come back to bite us on the ass," he said.

Little Tiger expected Bookman to be silenced by this rebuke, so she was shocked when he countered with his own sarcastic words. "What? Now you're sorry for making so much money on the side?"

"Well, no. I'm not complaining about that," said the Controller.

"Then shut your mouth!" said Bookman, waving his black ledger in the air.

Little Tiger stopped breathing. Never had she heard a Chinese man speak this way to his white boss.

And Bookman didn't stop there. "As long as this book matches payroll, names mean nothing to them. They don't know if we're dead or alive. All damn Chinamen are the same, right?"

Little Tiger hadn't moved but Bookman must have sensed she was there. He pushed aside some boxes and spied her through the opening.

"What do *you* want?" he asked in Chinese.

Little Tiger tried to answer nonchalantly as if she'd just now stumbled across the pair and had heard nothing. In Chinese she replied, "Oh, there you are. Powder asked me to find you."

The Controller looked at her ssuspiciously and turned to Bookman with a panicky expression. "What's he saying?" he asked.

Bookman shouted at Little Tiger. "Tell Powder I'll deal with him later. You, get back to work!"

With twitching fingers, the Controller lit a cigar. Little Tiger bowed to Bookman and ran off, more convinced than ever that he was not who he appeared to be.

The next morning as she was filling her tea pails, Bookman rode up on his horse and reined him in beside her.

"Little Tiger, you are no longer a tea boy."

She was so astounded she let the pails overflow.

"The Controller wants you on the explosives crew. He's seen what you can do and thinks you're wasted lugging tea pails."

Her wish had been granted! Little Tiger whipped off her apron and handed it to Powder. He rubbed what was left of his left arm. "Be careful, kid. Don't end up like me."

"Don't worry. I am fantastic with black powder," she answered.

"Damn it," he replied. "I'm already short of tea boys. Now I'm left with this shitload of work. Cooking, washing, cleaning, drying. Sonofabitch."

At the blasting site, the dynamite boss greeted Little Tiger's arrival with disdain. She figured it was because she had complained about the fuses being too short. Bookman marched her to the same swing chair she'd used to haul up Di Hong's body and she looked over the ledge to the foreboding scene below.

"This is your chair from now on, Xiao Hu. Learn from Wang Ma."

Little Tiger was offended. "I don't need to learn from him. I know what to do."

Bookman had no time for arrogance. "He survived the last accident. He can teach you something."

She stared at Bookman's face. "That scar. How did you get it?"

It seemed to Little Tiger that something switched in Bookman the minute she asked that question. Was it that he knew the work was dangerous and the little tea boy seemed too fragile for the work? Could this man possibly have a streak of human kindness? *Nonsense,* she thought. *This is a brutal man who can murder someone over a gold claim.*

"I got it from an accident," he answered guardedly. "Some accidents can change your life … or end it."

It was too much for Little Tiger to hold back her questions any longer. "They say you killed a man."

Bookman hardened. "That was an accident as well. Don't let any accident happen to you, Xiao Hu. Now do I have to tell you again to get to work?"

"No. I know what I have to do."

There were already a dozen men working on different parts of the cliff. Wang Ma was chiselling into the rock directly below and she descended in her own sling chair to work beside him. Her palms were sweating and her heart beating a thousand times a minute whenever she looked down into the swirling water far, far below. Huge boulders by the river's edge looked like pebbles from this distance. When she'd brought Di Hong's body up, she was so focused on the job that she hadn't had time to think about the danger she was in. When she squeezed through the hole in the tunnel and blasted it clear, she was thinking only of earning the five bucks. Never did she think then that her life might end with one small mistake. But now that her job was to blast away the side of a mountain, she realized that only her sling chair — three wooden slabs held together with ropes and connected by more rope to a hoist, kept her from a plunge into the river below — certain death.

She looked over to Wang Ma, hoping he would tell her not to be afraid, but instead he was deep in concentration. She chipped away at the rock with her chisel, trying to carve out a hole deep enough for a couple of sticks of dynamite.

"How much time do we have to set the charges?" she asked Wang Ma.

"As long as it takes. But if you make a mistake or the wind plays tricks on you, get yourself up to the top as fast as you can or you'll be blown all over the canyon."

Little Tiger looked at him in horror. He was pushing himself away from the cliff with his feet and twirling his chair like a kid on a swing.

"What are you doing?" she screamed.

"I'm a hawk!" he shouted, spreading his arms like wings and throwing his head back, laughing hysterically.

"Stop that!" she screamed, wanting to slap him across the face to bring him back to his senses.

He slowed down the twirling and gripped the rock face with his feet. He looked to the canyon, far below. "I think about that."

Little Tiger didn't understand. "Think about what?"

"Taking a jump, getting it over with. We're all going to die here, you know. Tiger, you'd send my bones home for me, wouldn't you?"

"Never talk like that. Never!" she screamed at him.

Wang Ma looked contrite. Little Tiger turned back to her work and pretended that all was well, but his words scared her.

They packed their dynamite sticks into the holes they'd made, lit their fuses, and called up the now-familiar cry "Fire in the hole!" The alarm bell rang and the hoist men at the top pulled with all their might to bring them up. Seconds later, they scrambled over the ledge just as explosions from their charges filled the air with smoke and dust. They spent the day working together, making more than a dozen cuts in the cliff. For the first time, Little Tiger felt that her work mattered.

As the sun set, she and Wang Ma wandered down the tracks with their grave markers.

"This is such a lonely place," said Little Tiger. "No families to mourn here, to set up altars and pray for the souls."

Wang Ma nodded solemnly.

"Someone should write the names and make sure their bones get back to their families," said Little Tiger.

Wang Ma said, "I thought Bookman did that and then the bone cleaner comes and sends the bones home."

"But maybe that doesn't happen all the time," said Little Tiger. "Maybe one of us should, to be double sure."

Wang Ma agreed. "You do it. You know how to write." He pointed to the new marker among them. "What does that one say?"

"You can't read at all?" asked Little Tiger.

"No. I never had a chance to learn."

"This is Di Hong's grave," she explained.

Wang Ma bowed three times to it.

Little Tiger walked between the rows of markers, reading out the other names. "This one is named Wu Kai, this one Bai Juan, this one Shen Tao, and this one …"

She stopped in her tracks and repeated the names aloud. Then, with a sudden realization, she turned and ran full steam back to the camp.

"What's wrong? What's so important?" shouted Wang Ma, but Little Tiger was long gone.

CHAPTER THIRTEEN

A light bulb lit up in Little Tiger's mind. Now she realized what the Bookman and the Controller were up to: they were cheating the company and lining their own pockets by keeping dead workers' names on the payroll and taking the money for themselves. Her instincts had been right from the beginning about that conniving Irishman, the Controller — and about Bookman. He must be as bad as she first thought. He was taking advantage of the Chinese, just like his white bosses did. Well, she was determined to end that.

She wanted to tell James about her realization, but he had taken his father off to Yale and she had no idea when he would be back. Who else could see that these crooks were exposed? Ah — Edgar, the engineer! He could. He was the right person to tell about their treachery. She ran to his work tent and waited until she was sure that he was alone, then shyly called in to him.

He was surprised to see the boy and furtively covered up the papers on his desk.

"I am sorry to bother you," said Little Tiger, "But I think there's something wrong with the ledger that Bookman keeps."

The engineer smiled at her as if she were daft. "Now what might that be?"

Little Tiger spun her tale. "I saw the names Wu Kai, Bai Juan, Shen Tao."

"Oh?" said Edgar. "So you can read and write. How admirable for a tea boy who is now our number-one explosives expert."

She continued, "I think Bookman does not remove the names of dead workers from his payroll when they die, and when it is pay time he takes their pay for himself and splits it with the Controller."

Edgar gasped. He seemed flabbergasted by her allegation. "So you think the Controller is in on this too?"

"I heard them. Maybe I'm wrong, but I don't think so."

Edgar scratched his chin. "My goodness! If this is true, it's terrible. I will look into it, but right now both Mr. Nichol and James have gone down to Yale. You haven't told this story to anyone, have you? Perhaps you mentioned it to James before he left?"

"No, I only found out now," she answered.

Edgar ran his hands down his vest. "I can't tell you how much I appreciate you bringing this to me. Don't mention it to a soul until I look into it. We wouldn't want to warn the guilty parties, would we? You can keep a secret, can't you?"

Little Tiger thought to herself, *I have kept more secrets than you will ever know.*

Edgar patted her on the shoulder and she left. But she had an intuition that something was very, very wrong.

A few days later, as the sun was rising above the eastern ridge, she heard the locomotive steam into the camp. Was it James bringing his father back from Yale? She wanted to see him, but things had changed between them and she had told the right person, Mr. Edgar, about the scam, so that could wait. And it did. It was several days until James came running after her as she headed toward the blasting site.

"I need to talk to you," he said, gripping her sleeve.

She yanked her arm away and ran along the track where the steam engine was sitting.

"Please," he called. "Let me explain."

He pulled her into the space between two railcars where no one could see them, took off his hat, and reached out to touch her face. She shied away from his touch and crossed her arms close to her chest.

"Is your father all right?" she asked.

"He's a stubborn old mule, but yes, he'll be fine."

Her lower lip trembled, fearing what he was about to say.

"Melanie is gone," he said. "Back to Victoria ... forever."

He leaned forward to kiss her. "I want to be with you," he whispered.

Li Jun turned her head. What was that sound? Was it someone behind the railcar? No, must be her imagination — it had stopped. She looked into James's eyes again.

So much to take in, tearing her apart inside. She spoke carefully. "I want to be with you too, James, but we come from two different worlds. I will always be a strange Chinese girl and you will always be son of boss."

He shook his head vehemently. "But why does that matter? I need you. I want you and I don't give a damn who else knows or what they think."

Little Tiger fought back tears. "Easy for you, easy for son of boss not to give a damn. Not easy for me."

"Who says we can't make a life together?"

"Who says?" She wiped away a tear. "Everyone."

"But I love you …"

Little Tiger put her finger to his lips. "I love you too, James, and one day maybe world will be better, people will care about what they share, not what makes them different, but now, for our lives, you can not be part of my world and I will never be part of yours."

"The hell with never! I'm talking about how I feel for you right now."

"Right now? What about two months or two years from now?"

James shook his head, confused.

Little Tiger explained. "Will you send me packing the way Mr. Relic sent his almost-wife packing?"

"No. I would never do that to you, I promise."

She shook her head sadly. "Mr. Relic was right. This way heartache lies. I do not want that for you, I care for you too much."

James reached for her. "Tiger …" he pleaded.

"My name is Li Jun."

"What?" said James. "I don't understand."

Her heart filled with sadness. "Li Jun is my real name. You don't even know who I really am. And I don't really know you." She turned away.

"Wait!" James called out but she ran off sobbing.

***

At the blasting site, Powder was ladling out the noodles. He called Little Tiger over and spoke to her sternly. "You need to be careful out there today."

"I am always careful," she replied. "I am fantastic with black powder, remember?"

Powder looked at the kid with knowing eyes and pointed to his sleeve, pinned up over the stump of his arm. "I was fantastic too," he said grimly.

Little Tiger wondered what prompted his warning.

Powder came closer. "Is there a reason the Controller would sneak into your tent? Is there something there for him to find? Something secret? Maybe gambling money, or stolen supplies?"

Little Tiger shook her head, confused. "I own nothing. Just my pay, and the Controller has no need for that bit of money." Then she frowned. What about the family photo, with her a little girl, hidden in her rucksack?

"What are you thinking about, kid?"

"Just a picture of my family from China when I was very young." She choked a bit. "When my mother was alive and my father was with us."

"The Controller is staggering around drunk, looking for Bookman and saying crazy things."

"What crazy things? "

"Crazy things like 'James brought a whore back from China.'"

"A whore?" screamed Little Tiger. Then, catching herself before she gave away everything, she joked, "Where does he keep her? Under his bed? Ha! We'd all know if there was a Chinese woman in the camp. Every man on our crew would be after her!"

Powder looked at her with pained eyes. "Okay, but warn Wang Ma that something is up. Maybe the Controller found something of his in the tent."

"Drink makes men crazy," said Little Tiger, trying to suppress her fears. What had the Controller discovered? Had Edgar already confronted him with her accusations? Was he now trying to discredit her by planting something he could accuse her of stealing? Maybe he didn't *take* something from the tent ... maybe he *put* something there. But what, she couldn't imagine. She looked around and saw Edgar giving instructions to the dynamite boss, who came over to her, grim-faced.

"Finish up your noodles and get to work," he snapped. Then he turned to Wang Ma. "Stay here. I need you up here on the ledge. The kid can go alone on this drop."

He grabbed Little Tiger's arm and pushed her onto her swing chair. Near the hoist, she saw the Controller come up to Bookman and throw his arm around him like a friendly drunk, then hand him something. Little Tiger couldn't see what it was, but it looked familiar. Bookman stared hard at it, then slipped it into his vest pocket and grabbed the Controller by the throat. But at that moment the hoist men started to lower her down the cliff and she could see nothing more.

Suddenly she realized — that was her family photo! Slip-sliding down in her swing chair, she heard Bookman scream. What was he saying? She couldn't hear over the creaking of the hoist and the roar of the river below. What were they doing up there on the ledge? Little Tiger sat stunned in her chair, knowing only one thing: something was terribly wrong and the faster she set her dynamite and lit the fuse, the faster she could call for the hoist men to bring her up. But to what? What would she face once she was on the ledge again?

Furiously, she chipped away at the granite. But then she heard her name being called. She looked up and saw Bookman leaning over the edge.

"Li Jun!" he screamed.

What? It was the first time anyone had called her Li Jun for years and years. Was she so frightened that her imagination was taking over? No. Again Bookman called "Li Jun," her real name. How could that be? In her confusion and fear only one answer came to her. Somehow he knew her father.

"Hold tight, Li Jun," he shouted. "We're pulling you up."

She lit the fuse and held on to her side ropes with both hands, waiting to be hoisted up. But with a sudden jerk, the wooden seat of her chair lurched to one side and dropped beneath her. What was happening? It felt as if the wooden slats were falling apart, as if the ropes holding them together were unravelling strand by strand. She was left with only the rope connecting her to the hoist. She clutched it with both her hands and stared up, too terrified to look down to the river waiting for her below.

"The ropes under your chair have been cut!" screamed Bookman. "I'm coming to get you."

And he leaped onto her rope and shimmied down. She held on, while her wooden seat dangled below her. It was no good to her now — hanging on to the hoist rope was her only hope. But her arms were giving out. They couldn't support her weight much longer. Her grip started to slip, and she prepared for the worst, but now Bookman was just above her on the rope.

"Give me your hand!" he shouted. "I'll support you."

Leaning against him, she got a few inches up the rope until they were holding each other, the two of them hanging on to the one rope.

Bookman looked scared. "You have to get higher. Climb up over me."

With her last bit of strength she placed her feet on Bookman's shoulder and boosted herself above him on the rope.

"Pull!" he screamed to the hoist men. The single rope groaned under the weight of the two of them. Inch by agonizing inch, they were lifted closer to the top of the cliff. She felt the furious beating of her heart and the tensing of the rope in her hands as she stood on Bookman's shoulders.

But at that moment the dynamite that she had set exploded. Little Tiger was thrown sideways like a rag doll, but she managed to hold on to her rope. Not Bookman. He was blown into the air, far off the cliff face. She watched as his body fell. Down, down it went and landed with a thud on a thin ledge far below.

Now she heard James's voice. Yes, that was him leaning over the ledge, terror in his eyes, ordering the hoist men to keep pulling her up.

"No," she called. "Send me down! Send me down!"

James stared at her, then called to the hoist men, "Do it!"

Slowly they released the winch so that Little Tiger could land on the ledge beside Bookman's limp body. She kneeled beside him. He was almost unconscious, badly wounded, blood seeping from the corner of his mouth onto the rocky ledge. She knew he was dying but she had to get to the truth and he was the only one who knew it. She grabbed hold of his shoulders with steely intensity.

"How do you know my real name? You must know where my father is. Tell me! The man you killed … was he my father?"

Bookman stared at her. He could hardly breathe and his eyes were glassy.

"Forgive me. I did not recognize my own daughter." He coughed up blood and gathered his last strength. His hand trembling, he reached into his vest pocket, pulled out the family picture, and handed it to her. "They told me you and your mother were dead. My child, can you forgive me?"

Li Jun stared at the familiar faces and then at Bookman. Yes, he was her father, in spite of his terrible scar! He had been here with her all this time and she hadn't known.

His eyes closed and his head rolled back. Li Jun lifted her head to the skies and uttered a terrible silent scream. She brought the photo up against her face, then collapsed with sobs that wracked her whole body.

Chapter Fourteen

Li Jun stuffed the photograph into her rucksack and watched as the hoistmen lifted Bookman's battered body to the surface. Then they lowered a chair for her.

As she ascended the mountainside, she replayed Bookman's death over and over in her mind. She heard him call her name — Li Jun! How brave he had been to crawl down the rope to save her. She thought of his dying words, the pain in his eyes when he realized that he hadn't recognized his own daughter. But this had been no accident. Someone had cut the ropes under her chair. The question was who? And why?

When she got to the top, she knelt beside Bookman's body and held his hand. She had been searching all this time for her father and he had been right beside her. She collapsed on his chest and wept, then took out the photograph and ran her fingers over her father's face

— the face of the man who became Bookman, scarred and bitter. She had found her father just in time to say goodbye to him.

Powder came to her side. He stared at the picture in her hand. "Is that Bookman's family? Hmm. I always thought he was a loner."

Li Jun nodded, but at first she didn't trust herself to speak. How many of the crew had heard Bookman cry out the name Li Jun and would guess her secret? Edgar, the Controller, and James — they all knew for certain. But how many others did? How many had seen Little Tiger respond to a girl's name, had witnessed Bookman rescue her on the cliff face? Probably many of them. There was no way now that she could stay on at the camp.

Powder shook his head sadly, watching the men lift the stretcher bearing Bookman's body. "Another man lost to the mountain."

When his body passed them, Li Jun and Powder both bowed in respect. Without a word, the entire crew followed their example.

"Powder, I have to tell you a secret. You must promise not to tell a soul."

He looked puzzled and she explained — she was the baby in the tintype photo and Li Man was her father.

"But this baby is a girl!" sputtered Powder.

"Yes," said Li Jun. "The only way I could find my father on Gold Mountain was to come disguised as a boy."

Powder scratched his head and examined her face with new eyes. "I often thought you were too pretty for a boy, but you were still a damn good worker."

"Keep my secret, please? At least until my father is buried."

"Of course," he said, and poked her arm. "You're still Little Tiger to me."

Li Jun smiled and looked around for James. There he was, standing beside the Controller. She ran to him.

"Thank God, you're safe," he said. "I heard Bookman call 'Li Jun' and I knew there was a big problem."

She stared hard at the Controller, cold as ice. "Why was Bookman attacking you on the ledge?"

The Controller stood mute, shuffling his feet, avoiding her eyes. James grabbed him by the collar and shouted, "Answer! A man's dead here. What do you know about it?"

"Wasn't my idea!" said the Controller. "We were after *her*."

Li Jun gasped and covered her mouth. James shook the Controller's shoulders till his head whipped back and forth. "You almost killed her, you little bastard!"

Li Jun piped up. "Somebody cut my ropes."

"Wasn't me," managed the Controller. "Edgar's the one who did that."

James released the Controller from his grip. "Edgar? My God! Do you mean that?"

Li Jun held up the photograph in front of the cowering man. "You stole this from my tent. Why?"

The Controller snarled. "You thought you were so clever, discovering our scam, but I heard ya having yer sweet talk with him between the railcars. Seemed mighty cozy for a tea boy and the boss's son, so I did some checkin' and sure enough, I found that picture in your tent. Saw that baby. You're a girl, aren't you? You can't hide it any more."

He looked at James and added snidely, "I figured that you'd pay good money to keep me from telling your father that this kid Little Tiger was actually your Little Whore."

Li Jun would have spit in the Controller's face, except that at that moment James threw a punch that landed on his cheek. The bone cracked and the Controller screamed.

"You wouldn't have made a cent," growled James. "I'm proud to be with her and I was about to tell my father."

"So, if that's the truth, are we gonna have a white wedding then?" snarled the Controller. "Oh, that's right! You China girls don't wear white. You wear red like the hootchy-kootchy girls."

James hit him again, on the other cheek.

Li Jun smiled wistfully. "See? Two different worlds. White is for death, not weddings. Red is for good fortune."

She turned to the Controller. "No wedding. People like you make sure we never be happy. But tell me, when did you know Bookman was my father?"

James and the Controller both sputtered. "What?"

Li Jun looked from one stunned face to the other. "Yes," she said, running her hands over the picture. "Bookman was my father. *He* was Li Man."

"So that's why he called out 'Li Jun!'" said James. "And why he climbed down the rope to save you. Your father gave his life for yours."

Li Jun nodded.

James tied the Controller's hands together. "Now you 'n' I are going to see Edgar," he said. "Come on, Li Jun. We both need to hear the whole story from him."

They marched the Controller down to the office car and cornered Edgar just as he was ripping pages out of Bookman's ledger.

"No you don't," said James. "You leave that evidence for the constables in Yale."

Edgar looked shaken. The Controller held out his tied hands. "The jig's up, m' lad."

Edgar looked at Li Jun and growled, "I knew you were trouble from the very first."

"Did you cut ropes under my chair? Did you?" she shouted.

"That I did, and it would have worked if Bookman hadn't played the hero."

"Did you know he was my father?"

"What!" Edgar slapped his thigh, amazed.

The Controller added, "Yep — Little Tiger is a girly girl and Bookman was her father."

"Well if that doesn't beat all. You goddamn Chinks!" said Edgar.

Li Jun explained to James the scam between Bookman, the Controller, and Edgar.

He turned to the two of them. "That about right? You were keeping dead men on the books and pocketing their pay? But why did you go after Little Tiger?"

"That kid was too smart. Figured it all out," said Edgar. "I put him on the explosives crew thinking he'd blow himself up, but he was too damn good. We had to do something that guaranteed he'd stay quiet — an accident while setting charges on the cliff, a chair collapsing beneath him. Nobody would guess it was murder. One more dead Chink fallen into the river, who would care?"

James was about to throw another punch but Li Jun put up her arm to stop him.

"Mr. Edgar, did Bookman know about your plan to kill me?"

The Controller and Edgar looked at each other. "No. He didn't even want to put you on the dynamite crew. He wanted to keep you safe."

Li Jun ran all the other questions through her mind. "Did he kill a man?"

"Yeah. Can't blame him," said Edgar. "Would've done the same myself. He worked hard in America, found himself a gold claim, but another Chinaman jumped it. Bookman wanted justice. The way I understand it, he hit the guy but it was a freak accident and he died, so Bookman came up here for a new beginning."

James interrupted. "But you held that over him, right? You blackmailed him 'cause he could be sent back to China for killing one of his own."

"How else do you think we got him to fix the books?" said Edgar nastily.

Now Li Jun had all the pieces to the puzzle. James tied up Edgar and the Controller, and left them in the office railcar for the police.

As she and James walked out together toward the camp, he shook his head. "My God, Li Jun! I can't believe everything that's happened. You were almost killed. Thank goodness Bookman got to you in time."

At the mention of her father's name, Li Jun brought her hands to her heart, then stopped in her tracks and clapped a hand over her mouth. "James. It was because of you!"

"What?"

"You heard my name and you came. You told the men to listen to me, to lower me down beside him."

"Against my better judgment. Imagine what could have happened."

"Something *very good* happened. I learned the truth about my father. I would never have known without you." Li Jun clasped his hands in hers. "Thank you, Mr. James."

He smiled. "Just James, remember?

"I'm sorry your father died. You spent so long looking for him and had so little time with him. I want to help you plan his burial, but first I have to tell *my* father about those two crooks and make arrangements for the Mounties to lock them up."

"That is good ... James. But me — I am not sure what to do. I promised my *Ama* that I would bring back my father's bones to bury beside her, but I have been thinking ..." Li Jun chewed her bottom lip.

James put his hands on her shoulders. "What is it?"

"How do I know bone cleaner will come for his body? It will be many years, maybe five or six, till he comes, if he comes at all, and I will not be here. Even then, how do I know my father's bones will really go back to his village?"

James thought long and hard. "You're right. There is another way. We could arrange to cremate your father. Powder will know how to do it properly, with all respect."

She had been thinking the same thing. If her father's body could be cremated, she could keep her promise. After the ceremony, she could place the ashes and unburned bones in an urn and take them to Victoria by train. Powder would know someone there who could make sure that the bones went back to China, to her village. Her mother and father would be together again — just as her mother wished.

She looked into James's blue, blue eyes and threw her arms around him.

"Thank you, thank you, James. That is best."

But still, she scrunched her brow.

"Don't worry," he said. "I'll arrange for an honourable ceremony and see that you have a fine urn. And I want to pay for getting it back to China."

Li Jun knew that she was not going back to her village. Canada was her home now. But all she said was, "No, I want to pay for that. I have saved enough." She bowed to him with an enormous sense of relief.

***

Flames leaped from the funeral pyre that was prepared for her father. Li Jun knelt beside it wearing her mourning band around her head. Together with James and Powder, she threw spirit money into the fire. It was so intense that she couldn't really see her father's body disappearing but she felt that his spirit was rising, free because soon he would lie beside his wife in their ancestral village.

Nevertheless she felt a deep sadness. *All along he was near to me every day*, she thought, *here in the camp — my own father! I hated him and his scar and what I thought he had done. If only I'd known, I could have told him about my mother and me, our life after he left us, how much we longed for him. At least I know that his soul will not wander, searching for his wife and his homeland.*

***

James stayed close to her during her days of mourning and she still had many questions.

"Tell me, James, why would Bookman go along with cheating you and your father by paying the dead workers and keeping the money?"

"I don't really know," he answered. "Those two could have got him hanged. Or maybe he thought it was his due. Maybe he planned to give the money to the families of the dead men. We don't send their pay back home when they die here. We take them for granted. They're honest and hard-working but we … we don't keep our promises to them."

Li Jun nodded her head. "I know. No one told us we would be paid less than the white workers. No one told us we would have to pay back our passage. No one told us we could die here."

James nodded, and put his arms around her. "Our part of the railway is almost done."

"And done on time," she added.

"Thanks to you. You really *do* explode fantastic!"

She laughed. But then her laughter turned to tears. Over and over she had wrestled with the biggest question of all: could she make a life with this white man, rich and privileged, whose world was so different from hers, whose family would be appalled at the idea of him marrying her? Did they *really* know each other? They'd had so little time alone, most of the moments stolen. He didn't even know her real name till a day ago.

She thought of Powder's advice — "Never trust the *gwailo*" — and of Bookman, her own father's, warning — "Their friendship means nothing; only Chinese look after Chinese."

Yes, James had changed since their first meeting. Yes, she had opened his mind and heart to care about her and her Chinese friends, but how long would that last? Again she thought of Mr. Relic's advice: "Look, but never touch. That way heartache lies." He had loved his Chinese almost-wife but her family despised him, his own world shunned him, and he had abandoned her. Surely that was what awaited James and her. His promises were comforting, but reality was another matter.

However, she could not go back to China. There she had nothing and no one, while in this new country, with her courage and skills, she had a future — even as a woman. She made her decision.

"I must leave," she said. "Leave you and make my own way."

"Leave? No! I want you to stay. I want to make a life with you."

"I have to go," she murmured.

"Then I will go with you."

Li Jun smiled sadly. She knew in her heart that it could not be. "That is an impossible dream, James. You think we can change the world, but I think it more likely the world changes *us*. I have dreams of my own. Maybe I go to school in Victoria. Powder say times are changing. He hear that some Chinese women are coming here. They work in restaurants and in laundries. Maybe there's a fireworks factory! There *are* mission schools. Who knows, maybe one day I can be a teacher. My father was a teacher, you know? I will go my own path and you will stay here to finish the railroad."

James was speechless, heartbroken. He reached out to her but she stepped back. She longed for his arms around her, but instead she smiled sadly and turned away. Her future was not with him.

***

In her tent, Li Jun packed her few belongings and the money she'd saved into her satchel, picked up the urn with her father's bones, and walked through the camp toward the waiting train. She passed workers setting out for the tunnels, the bridges, and the tracks. She hoped their lot might be better now with Edgar and the Controller gone.

Wang Ma was the last of them. He stopped in front of her and threw his hands in the air. "Powder told me you're leaving."

"Is that the only thing he said?"

"Well, no — he complained again about the rice and the noodles, then said that no one can make tea like you, that you must sneak in some magic potion he doesn't know about."

Li Jun laughed, then quickly changed her tone. "Wang Ma, prepare for a shock. I am going to tell you something that I have hidden from you all this time."

"I think I know," he said. "When I heard Bookman call you Li Jun, I remembered long ago a little girl in my village with that name."

Li Jun was amazed and stared into his eyes. "So you know why I am leaving. I cannot stay here as a woman."

Wang Ma cocked his head and looked at her as if seeing her in a whole new way.

She gave him a friendly poke in the ribs. "Stop that!"

He returned the poke and smiled. "Who would have guessed that under that hat and all that grime, you were such a good-looking woman?"

Li Jun felt a blush rise to her cheeks.

Then Wang Ma spoke from his heart. "Li Jun, you'll always be my best friend. That day on the cliff, you saved my life. You gave me hope that things would get better. I owe you a debt."

"Then come to Victoria one day and buy me a bean cake," she quipped.

Wang Ma teased her. "My life is worth only a bean cake?"

She grinned. "I'm going to miss your jokes, Wang Ma. Please take care of yourself. It's still dangerous here but when you finish the job, I hope you'll come to Victoria and start a new life there, like I'm going to do."

Now serious, Wang Ma stepped closer to her. "I will come and find you," he promised. Li Jun felt he was about to hug her but at that moment she spotted James.

"Make sure you do, Wang Ma!" she called out as she ran to James for one last goodbye.

"At least let me walk you to the train," James said.

They arrived beside the steam engine and she whispered, "I need you to hold me one last time."

He put his arms around her and she felt him tremble in that long embrace.

The sharp sound of the whistle signalled that the train was about to leave. Li Jun released herself from his arms, picked up the urn with her father's ashes, and walked to the open railcar. It was the same railcar she had arrived in and this time it seemed an endless walk. When she arrived, she turned for a last look at James. He stood tall, but he was shaking. She climbed up onto the railcar just as she had climbed down from it when she first came to Hell's Gate. Slowly the train wheels began to move, the great locomotive belched smoke and began to steam along the tracks. Li Jun held her father's funeral urn close to her heart. She didn't turn to look at James, afraid that she might change her mind and leap off the train to go back to him. She was not the girl who had left China on her quest. But she was not Little Tiger either.

She could hardly wait to take off her slouch hat and throw away the bindings that had hidden her secret for so many years. Now she could stop all that cursing and swaggering. She could walk like the woman that James had shown her she could be. It would be scary — but also exciting. She imagined herself in a beautiful gown just like the one her mother wore in the family picture and let out a huge sigh.

Things were going to be all right. Powder had arranged for someone to send her father's bones back to her village and James, thoughtful James, had arranged for a family he knew in Victoria to let her live with them until she could find work. Already she was dreaming of soaking in a tub of hot water and scrubbing the mountain dust away.

She cradled the urn more tightly. *Rest, Father. Rest well in China beside Mother. I will stay here to make a new life in this new land. You taught me to be first class, and showed me that life must be lived with a fire in my soul. Thank you, Father.*

Li Jun looked ahead. The rails seemed to stretch forever in front of her, and she knew that her true journey was just beginning.

Historical Afterword

The railway was completed in 1885. Immediately after that, the Canadian government imposed a head tax on all Chinese immigrants, which prevented most of the Chinese railway workers from bringing their families to join them in Canada.

Even so, $23 million was collected from this tax — 1.2 billion in today's dollars — more than it cost to build the entire railway.

In 2006 the government finally issued an official apology to Chinese Canadians for the head tax.

Three Chinese workers died for every mile of track they laid.

Of Related Interest

Kootenay Silver
Ann Chandler

In 1910, while twelve-year-old Addy McLeod waits in a cabin in the Kootenay wilderness of southeastern British Columbia for her brother, Cask, to send for her, she fends off the unwanted advances of her alcoholic stepfather. When tragedy strikes, she is forced to flee and disguise herself as a boy.

Addy's determined search for Cask becomes a journey of self-discovery as she encounters a tough trapper woman who cares for her when she's ill, works in a hotel in the silver town of Kaslo on Kootenay Lake, and meets her first love, Ian.

But just as Addy's search for Cask is about to end, the First World War breaks out and her world is torn apart once again. With great resolve she devotes herself to joining the war effort on the home front and eventually learns what forgiveness is all about.

In Search of Sam
Kristin Butcher

Raised by her mother, eighteen-year-old Dani Lancaster only had six weeks to get to know her father, Sam, before he lost his battle with cancer. It was long enough to love him, but not long enough to get to know him — especially since Sam didn't even know himself.

Left on the doorstep of an elderly couple when he was just days old, and raised in a series of foster homes, Sam had no idea who his parents were or why they had abandoned him. Dani is determined to find out. With nothing more than an address book, an old letter, and a half-heart pendant to guide her, she sets out on a solo road trip that takes her deep into the foothills, to a long-forgotten town teeming with secrets and hopefully answers.